CITY
OF GRIT
AND GOLD

Maud Macrory Powell

 ALLIUM PRESS OF CHICAGO

Allium Press of Chicago
Forest Park, IL
www.alliumpress.com

This is a work of fiction. Descriptions and portrayals of real people, events, organizations, or establishments are intended to provide background for the story and are used fictitiously. Other characters and situations are drawn from the author's imagination and are not intended to be real.

Book and cover design by E. C. Victorson

Front cover images:
(top) unidentified girl, photographer: Elmer Chickering, Boston
(bottom) "The Anarchist Riot in Chicago,"
Harpers Weekly, May 15, 1886

ISBN: 978-0-9967558-5-6

Library of Congress Cataloging-in-Publication Data

Names: Powell, Maud Macrory, author.
Title: City of grit and gold / Maud Macrory Powell.
Description: Forest Park, IL : Allium Press of Chicago, [2017] | Summary: Addie, a twelve-year-old Jewish girl in 1886 Chicago, struggles to keep her family together at the time of the Haymarket affair, as laborers protest for better working conditions.
Identifiers: LCCN 2016058524 (print) | LCCN 2017015768 (ebook) | ISBN 9780996755863 (Epub) | ISBN 9780996755856 (pbk.)
Subjects: LCSH: Haymarket Square Riot, Chicago, Ill., 1886--Juvenile fiction. | Labor movement--Illinois--Chicago--Juvenile fiction. | CYAC: Haymarket Square Riot, Chicago, Ill., 1886--Fiction. | Labor movement--Fiction. | Jews--United States--Fiction. | Immigrants --Fiction. | German Americans--Fiction. | Family life--Illinois--Chicago--Fiction. | Chicago (Ill.)--History--19th century--Fiction.
Classification: LCC PZ7.1.P694 (ebook) | LCC PZ7.1.P694 Ci 2017 (print) | DDC [Fic]--dc23
LC record available at https://lccn.loc.gov/2016058524

This book is dedicated to my children—
Grace, treasure of my heart, and Sam, my little bear

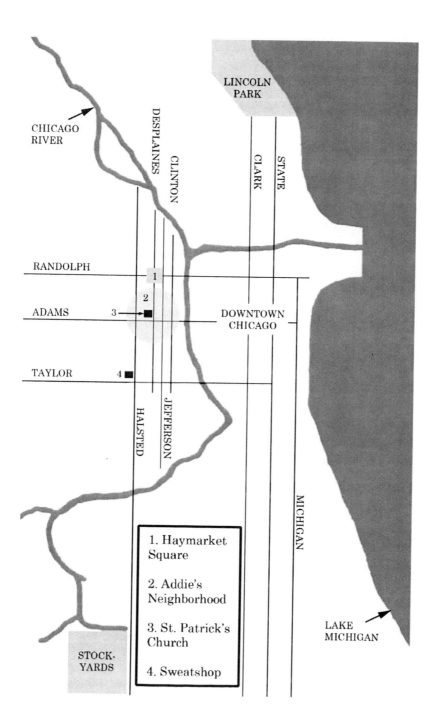

CHICAGO
RIVER

LINCOLN
PARK

DESPLAINES

CLINTON

CLARK

STATE

RANDOLPH

1

2

ADAMS   3

DOWNTOWN
CHICAGO

TAYLOR   4

HALSTED

JEFFERSON

MICHIGAN

1. Haymarket
Square

2. Addie's
Neighborhood

3. St. Patrick's
Church

4. Sweatshop

STOCK-
YARDS

LAKE
MICHIGAN

City of Grit and Gold

One

April 1886

THE WHOLE city of Chicago seemed to be holding its breath, waiting. Streets were emptier than usual and the stores lonely for customers. Addie fingered the thick, silky ribbon on a brown suede derby as she sat by herself in the hat shop. The shop felt small and cramped, with dark walnut shelves of men's hats lining three walls and a square wooden table in the middle, on which women's feathery hats were displayed on wire stands. After school she minded the shop while her papa and his brother, Uncle Ehud, went to the bank or out on other business. She preferred when the shop was full of customers to watch and interact with—she would try to imagine their lives at home and what their children looked like and how they had come to live in Chicago. But today felt boring and lonely, and Addie wished time would hurry up.

Sighing, she returned the derby to its shelf and picked up a women's gray hat, the kind worn by the fanciest ladies on State Street. The narrow, elegant brim was adorned with a massive ostrich plume. She peeked out the window, up and down the streets for Uncle Ehud. With the coast clear, she perched the hat on top of her head and admired herself in the shop's mirror. Addie was only twelve years old but tall for her age. Her large brown eyes took in everything around her. She tried to make herself look regal and rich, with her nose tilted up and an expression of dissatisfaction around her mouth, but then stuck her tongue out at herself and giggled. Next she pulled a shiny black bowler off the shelf and tried it on. Wearing this hat made her stand up taller. She closed her eyes and imagined riding in a horse-drawn carriage, parading along Lake Michigan at a fast clip.

The shop bell jangled, as Uncle Ehud returned to close up for Shabbat. He seemed distracted and hardly noticed as Addie quickly returned the bowler to its spot on the bottom shelf. Bowlers and derbies on the bottom, then caps and beanies on the next shelf up, top hats on the top shelf of course, and on the third shelf right at eye level, all the latest fashions—the porkpies and straw boaters and sailor hats. "Remember to pick up the challah for supper," he mumbled, handing Addie some coins and disappearing into the store room. "I'll be along with the boys in a bit."

—◦—

Addie stood in front of the bakery hugging the warm loaves against her, not ready to go home quite yet. She loosened the ties of her calico bonnet, letting her long brown braids fall down her back. But she was careful to keep her head covered while still on the street. Half a block away, Widow Adler sat on the front stoop of their apartment building in her spindle-legged chair and looked down the street, like a hungry eagle ready to pounce on an unsuspecting mouse. Addie dreaded speaking to her because her skin and breath reeked of garlic and vinegar. She lingered another moment but, knowing that Papa would worry if she stayed away too long, forced herself to keep walking.

She longed to nibble on the sweet bread in her arms. Mama had chided her to leave the loaves whole for Shabbat. Though she'd eaten a whole bowl of lamb and potato stew at the noon meal, her stomach rumbled greedily. Papa said she was growing like a weed this year, already taller than her sister, Miriam, who was four years older.

Shabbat fell every Friday, and that meant Addie might be home for two whole days in the tight apartment, sewing or studying or helping Mama. Sometimes, if there was no work to do on Sunday after temple, Addie could go to her friend Greta's apartment to play. Usually she moved fast, the great Chicago wind thrumming against her skin, but now she dragged along like molasses. She waved to the widow and kept her head down, hoping not to be addressed.

"Slow down, girl," the old woman called in her sharp-warm voice and Addie felt her stomach tighten. *Go over and be polite.* Moving quickly now, she held her breath and bent down to kiss the widow's cheek, which was wrinkled and hardened by decades of working under a strong sun in Germany, the old country. "Go home now, before your Papa misses you," the widow urged. "There's trouble in this city and your parents shouldn't let you run around as they do."

Addie's ears pricked. *Trouble in the city?* Chicago was crowded with noisy men, skinny horses, heaps of trash, and children with smudged, drawn faces. Tall buildings filling up the open sky. *More trouble than all of that?* Questions caught in Addie's throat.

"Go on, now," the widow repeated, and Addie swallowed her questions and hurried up the stairs.

Two

A DDIE'S FAMILY had moved from Germany to Chicago in the hopes of finding a better, more peaceful life. Papa came thirteen years ago, when Mama was still pregnant with Addie. He joined Uncle Ehud at the hat shop and secured a place to live and made sure the new country would be safe and suitable for his family. When Addie was four the rest of the family traveled first by boat and then by train to the great city of Chicago. Addie hardly remembered the journey. She could only feel Mama holding her through the long nights at sea, as the waves churned beneath their boat. She smelled the salty air and felt the crowds push up against her in a kind of fervor that frightened her.

When Addie swung open the front door, Papa was speaking to Mama in his quiet-cold voice in the front room. "...not welcome here as long as he's involved—" He stopped speaking. Mama whisked the challah from Addie and retreated into the kitchen. Papa's great nostrils flared, a sure sign he was angry, but he swallowed hard, as though trying to put the anger away. Papa was broad and strong like an ox, with beetle brown eyes and wiry whiskers growing all over his chin and cheeks.

Addie's heart fluttered in her chest. Papa and Mama rarely disagreed in words, putting their arguments carefully inside long silences and pursed lips. *Who's not welcome here? My brother, Moshe? Papa's brother, Ehud? Mama's brother, Chaim?* Addie prayed they were not speaking of her Uncle Chaim.

Unlike the other adults, who were forever busy and worried, Uncle Chaim played games with Addie. He was tall and handsome, with eyes like hazelnuts, and a trimmed beard of soft brown. When she was younger, and he'd first arrived by train from New York, he'd pretend to be a fierce brown bear from the Black Forest. He would growl and crawl around on his hands and knees until Addie shrieked and ran down the hall to the back bedroom to hide. He would throw her over his shoulder like a sack of grain, or pull her braids while she tried to sew her sampler, and called her *bärchen*, his little bear. Since she'd grown too tall for baby games, they played the card game *Elfern* in the front room where Uncle Chaim slept at night. He would tell stories about his days working on the railway—the lines of cars stretching across the plains and over the horizon—that brought people and goods to the heap of Chicago.

Mama had already set out the candles and laid the lace tablecloth for Shabbat. Uncle Chaim, and also Uncle Ehud with his eight-year-old twin sons David and Sammy, would join them at dusk for the evening meal.

Papa stared out the window, his eyes narrowed. He took hold of the tape measure around his neck, the tape that measured men's heads in the hat shop, and pulled it with each hand, alternating so that the tape slid back and forth along his shoulders. He reminded Addie of the marmalade cat living behind their apartment, scratching its back against a hitching post. Papa hardly noticed Addie. She was relieved, as he usually asked her a hundred sharp questions about where she'd been. But she felt frightened, too. Papa didn't seem like himself. Addie slipped into the tiny kitchen with Mama.

A worried crease stood out on Mama's forehead, pulsing with unspoken feeling. She opened the oven and pulled out the *kugel*, a noodle dish colored bright yellow from fresh egg yolks and flecked green with bitter parsley leaves. Addie's mouth watered and she forgot Mama's worries for a moment.

5

Mama bit her lip, then looked up at Addie. "Tell me what you saw today." Her voice sounded tight. Unlike Greta's mother, Mrs. Raczynski, Mama rarely left the apartment, as her joints ached with rheumatism and climbing the stairs left her in pain for days. She stayed in the apartment cooking and cleaning and taking in sewing from neighbors to pay for Miriam and Moshe's extra books, while Addie eagerly ran errands for her.

"St. Patrick's church is being repaired on Adams Street, with workmen buzzing about like bees and lines of scaffolding..." Addie prattled on, watching to see if the crease in Mama's forehead would soften and disappear as she spoke. "And I saw a crowd of men standing outside a building on Halsted Street yelling things with their fists raised." She paused. "Mama, is it true that the workers in Chicago will begin striking next week if they're not given an eight-hour workday?" Her teacher, Miss Green, had mentioned the strikes at the end of the school day.

Mama turned away and began to stir the chicken broth on the stove. "Take the plates to the table now, Addie." The crease in her forehead had returned and her round face was flushed.

Addie couldn't tell if the heat from the stove made Mama look so hot or if she'd said something wrong again. *Why can't I keep my mouth shut?* Her throat tightened and her face prickled. In her haste to get the plates, the top one slipped and almost crashed to the floor. Oh, how she longed to be out on the streets again where she could move her long limbs without fear of breaking anything! *Uncle Chaim will be here soon and then everything will feel right again.*

In the front room Addie carefully set the plates on the long table. Papa was still looking out the window and she made a game of moving as slowly and quietly as possible, so as not to attract his attention. The challenge of being perfectly silent buoyed her spirits for a moment and, when she finished, she tiptoed back into the kitchen. "Mama, I forgot to tell you about a new shop—" The footfalls of heavy boots meant that Uncle Chaim was climbing the apartment stairs. Addie's heart lifted and her chest grew warm.

But, before she could open the kitchen door and race to greet him, Mama grabbed her arm and pulled her in close.

"Help me clean these pots. My back is aching terribly." Addie began to protest but Mama put her finger to her lips and said, "*Bitte schweigen!* You must stay quiet. Hush, child!"

Addie took a wire brush and began to scrub the large stew pot. She pushed her frustration down through the brush, focused on scrubbing the brown stains until gray metal appeared from beneath.

In the next room, Papa and Uncle Chaim spoke in brittle-hot tones. Addie strained to make out the words. Papa's voice rose in spurts. "In a capitalistic country…no room for…engine of commerce…" Uncle Chaim's deep voice rumbled like distant thunder, his words indecipherable. Mama began to rock back and forth. Addie looked at her for reassurance but Mama's eyes were latched onto the wooden spoon in her hand.

The front door slammed and Papa shouted, "*Verdammt!*"

Mama sucked in her breath and rushed out to Papa, leaving the kitchen door open. "Where did he go? Did you send him away?" she implored. "All this is only politics and here we are in a new country with so little left of our family. Oh, Josef, what have you done?"

Addie cringed inside, wanting to follow Uncle Chaim down the steps and onto the street.

"How long will this be a new country to you?" Papa bellowed. "We are Americans now and this is our country. Chaim joined the Knights of Labor even after my warnings—the unions and anarchists plan to swallow your new country whole or set Chicago into another blazing inferno!"

Moshe appeared from the back bedroom carrying a newspaper. His curly brown hair looked rumpled. "What's happened? Mama? Papa?" Miriam emerged as well. Addie stayed perfectly still behind the kitchen door and listened. She didn't want to remind them of her presence, in case they were trying to hide something from her. *I wish I understood why Papa's so angry with Uncle Chaim.*

7

"Please, Josef." Mama stifled a sob, the anger gone from her voice. "He's our family. He's *my* family. Please let this go."

Though she hated to hear Mama beg, Addie felt desperate, too. She waited for more words, but the front door opened and in tumbled Sammy and David with Uncle Ehud just behind. Addie ran through the kitchen door to her cousins, who hugged her around the waist and showed her the kite Uncle Ehud had bought them. Mama and Miriam fled to the kitchen, while Papa and Moshe sat down at the table with Uncle Ehud and spoke together in hushed voices. Addie felt lost. She was neither adult nor child but caught somewhere between the two, by herself. The boys were delighted to see her, so she admired their kite and asked them about school.

David and Sammy made an unusual pair. Though they were identical looking, David laughed easily and bounded about like the ringmaster in a circus, while Sammy was shy and thoughtful. Tonight, however, Sammy showed off the kite while David watched. David began to cough and Addie noticed how pale he looked. "And look how long the tail is!" Sammy exclaimed, and Addie felt her heart grow lighter. She loved the two boys who wanted to play and run around and looked to her for direction, as though her opinion mattered. Just before sundown, Mama lit the Shabbat candles and Papa made the Kiddush and said the blessing over the challah. Mama served the kugel and broth and challah and carrots glazed in molasses and butter, but Addie found that she had little appetite. David coughed again and Uncle Ehud scolded him for drinking his broth too quickly. While the family shared news of the day and Uncle Ehud and Papa discussed the hat shop, no one mentioned Uncle Chaim. Addie felt his absence like a hole torn in the side of her winter coat, with cold air seeping in and making her heart feel numb. Though surrounded by her family, and mountains of food and the warmth of the Shabbat candles, she felt hollow inside. She wondered if Uncle Chaim would return home later to sleep in his usual place on the sofa. *Where is he now? And where, if not here, will he sleep tonight?*

Three

DAVID CONTINUED to cough at the table, in spells that grew longer. His dark eyes, set close together like a monkey's Addie had once seen in a book from the Zoological Society, stayed shut even when he wasn't coughing. Mama and Uncle Ehud eyed each other without speaking or smiling and Addie wondered if David was in trouble for taking so much attention during Shabbat. Then Mama brought him a cup of water and stroked his head while he tipped back to drink. Mama was not angry. But the drink was useless, and the coughing took over again, growing louder and more demanding. Addie wished David would stop.

Moshe spoke to Papa and Uncle Ehud again. "The railways have become..." but then waited to continue, the coughing so loud now that no one could really hear him. Addie looked back at David and noticed, with a jolt that ran across her shoulders and down the length of her spine, a patch of blood shaped like an angry star spattered on his handkerchief. Dark red spread through the fine cotton threads.

A moment later, Mama stood up and pulled David's chair out from the table. "Ehud, this boy must go to bed," she said. So, without a word, Uncle Ehud picked him up and carried him to the back bedroom. David looked tiny against his father's wide shoulders and broad back. Though Ehud was not a very tall man, he was built like a stout pony that could carry more than its own weight over a mountain.

Miriam trailed behind Mama, murmuring quietly, "What should I do? Should I boil the kettle?" Miriam was only a bit taller than Mama, but her shape was a whisper in comparison. Now that she was sixteen, she wore grown-up dresses that fell below her ankles and seemed to swallow her up.

"Yes," Mama replied in a low voice. "Put the kettle on and make some tea for David and bring me a rag dipped in cold water."

Addie wanted to get up and help, too, to make herself useful like Mama and Miriam, but her legs felt numb and cold.

When Uncle Ehud returned, Papa leaned forward in his chair. "How long has David been coughing this way? He should see a doctor at once." Papa sounded angry, like he was accusing his brother of not taking proper care of his son.

"He was up last night coughing but seemed well enough to go to school today." Uncle Ehud stood slowly. "This is the first I've seen blood." He walked toward the hall to the back bedroom, like he was listening for Mama to call him but didn't really want to go. The kettle groaned. Mama hummed quietly and Miriam scuttled to get the kettle, but there was no sound of coughing. Uncle Ehud looked at the floor. "If only Rebecca was still alive. These poor boys need a mother. This city is so full of garbage and filth and illness." His shoulders sagged and Addie felt sad, a fretful pain clawing at her throat.

Sammy sat next to Addie with his hands together and little fingers wriggling around each other like earthworms, his eyebrows raised high and lips pursed in a scrunched letter O. He was looking at Addie, who recognized the signal. Sammy wanted Addie to find an excuse to go play. Her mind raced. They couldn't play in the back bedroom, and night had fallen, so there was nowhere to go.

Meanwhile, Papa ignored his brother's mention of his late wife and suggested that they find the doctor at once. "David should be seen by Dr. Goldstein tonight." He paused. "Don't you agree, Ehud?"

Funny that Papa looks for Uncle's approval, even though he seems so sure of what David needs, Addie thought. Uncle Ehud was Papa's older brother by five years and, even when Papa seemed so strong and certain, he always wanted Uncle Ehud's approval.

The coughing started up again and Addie felt dread rise through her middle, like icy liquid bubbling upward. Miriam emerged from the kitchen carrying a mug of tea that looked like it must have been too full. She was tiptoeing along the hallway, trying to make sure it wouldn't spill onto her hands. Addie imagined the tea burning her own fingers and, with the chill still up in her chest, she desperately wanted to leave the room with Sammy. *Burning and chilling, burning and chilling—sure signs of illness on its way,* Addie thought with a shudder. Uncle Ehud stood by the front door, tugging on his snowy beard and nodding at Papa, silently agreeing that David needed to see the doctor.

"Moshe, take your coat and go get Dr. Goldstein. Tell him about David's illness and ask him to come see the boy," Papa said in his bossy-loud voice. No one spoke or moved. Moshe had contracted polio as a boy, back in Germany, the year before Addie was born. Addie had always known his leg was bad, but Mama hadn't told her about the illness until last year when Addie had talked about seeing a crippled girl at the market. Mama explained that Moshe had almost died and then stayed in bed for four months. His leg was ruined by the illness, so he walked with a deep limp and his whole body ached if he moved too much. Mama would rub camphor oil on his leg on bad nights, while he gritted his teeth.

Had Papa forgotten Moshe's leg? Or perhaps he was testing Moshe, to see if his leg was getting stronger now that he was almost eighteen. Addie watched Moshe to see what he would say. It didn't seem possible that Moshe could find his way to Dr. Goldstein's at night. From the time Addie was seven or eight Papa and Mama had sent her out to do errands. Small ones at first—picking up challah from the baker across the street or asking a neighbor for

11

a pinch of salt. Addie would button up her coat and put on her hat before Mama had finished asking, that was how eager she'd been to leave the apartment. Miriam liked to help in the kitchen best or read books or sew. And Mama made excuses for Moshe to stay home to protect his leg.

Moshe rose from his chair and looked at Addie. "Which is the quickest way to the doctor's house?" he asked.

Addie's face flushed. None of this seemed fair. She wanted to leave and yet Moshe, who could barely walk to school and find his way to the butcher, was going. But Papa's jaw was set. Addie would have to endure David's pitiful coughing and the worried adults and poor Sammy, who looked like a trapped animal.

She forced herself to speak. "Make a left outside and take the bakery alley, then right onto Adams, past the horse stable and the old bank, and then right again on Clinton Street until you pass the tavern. Dr. Goldstein's house is next to the cloth shop on the left."

"Should I go, too, Papa?" Sammy asked, his hands disappearing under the table.

"No, son," Uncle Ehud replied. "You stay here with me and Addie. You mustn't be outside in the night." His voice sounded sad and miserable.

Sammy looked at the food on his plate but his hands stayed under the table.

"Hurry up, Moshe." Papa's voice was impatient and gravelly.

Moshe pulled his coat from a hook by the door very slowly, almost as if he was expecting Mama to rush down the hall and make things right. *Why can't Papa or Uncle Ehud fetch the doctor?* Addie thought. *They're old and creaky and complain about the apartment steps, but surely Papa's pushing Moshe too much...* Before she finished this thought the door shut behind Moshe and he was gone.

Addie caught Sammy's eye and stuck her tongue out at him quickly, like a lizard, so that Papa and Uncle Ehud wouldn't see. Sammy smiled and crossed his eyes, tilting his head at the same time so he looked like a happy fool. The tightness in Addie's chest loosened. At least she could keep Sammy amused from across the table. Next she opened her eyes very wide and pulled her chin and mouth down so that her face became skinny and long like the letter I. Mama emerged from the back room with Miriam trailing behind her.

"He's beginning to run a fever and his pulse is very fast. I hope Dr. Goldstein arrives soon." She spoke in a quiet-soft voice to Papa and Uncle Ehud, though the rest of the family could hear every word. "He shouldn't be moved," she continued. "You and Sammy stay here for the night." She pointed her chin at the spot where Uncle Chaim usually slept, her face showing nothing of how she felt about this one uncle sleeping in the place of the other.

Addie's stomach clenched and her mind wandered back to Uncle Chaim. *Where could he be, now?*

"Let's wait and see what Dr. Goldstein says. Three more of us here, and with David so ill…" Uncle Ehud's voice trailed off.

Mama placed her hand on his arm. "He must rest, *bruder*. You cannot risk taking him out into the night."

Uncle Ehud looked tired, his eyes crinkled almost shut as he leaned against the wall and pulled his beard. Addie turned back to Sammy. "Shall we play pinochle after the plates are cleared and the washing done?" Sammy nodded and smiled, but his eyes shifted about the room nervously.

As Addie stood up to take plates back to the kitchen, the apartment door opened and there stood Moshe, panting and shaking his head.

"Addie! I couldn't find it," he spat out, as he glared at her. She could hear the blame and anger mounting in the sound of her name. "You told me to turn right on Clinton and it would be next to the cloth shop. There's no cloth shop there. Are you sure I was supposed to turn right on Clinton?"

Addie felt trapped by the question. Papa and Mama and Uncle Ehud waited for her to respond. There was no winning. Either way, one of them would be wrong, and then Papa would lash out. Addie shut her eyes and found the map inside her head. Ever since she could remember she'd been able to picture the neighborhood in her mind's eye. Crisscrossing streets and alleys appeared behind her eyelids, with a bright red line marking the path for her to take. She could see the line to Dr. Goldstein's house—Adams Street, wide and friendly, and Clinton, narrower but still friendly, and the alley, a bit evil looking but fast and useful. The lines crossed each other in a neat grid. She opened her eyes. "Yes, Moshe. Right on Clinton and next to the cloth shop."

Moshe threw up his hands and huffed, then he turned to Papa and Uncle Ehud. "I couldn't find it. I'm sorry."

The crease stood out on Mama's forehead. "Addie'll have to go. There's no choice. David's gravely ill and we need the doctor."

Papa began to say something but then stopped himself.

"I'll go back with her," Moshe piped up. "My leg's all right and now I'm determined to see where the doctor's house is."

Addie looked at her family, at Mama whose knees were so bad she could barely walk down the stairs, and Papa and Uncle Ehud who seemed bewildered by the whole city except for home and temple and the hat shop, and Moshe who was half-crippled, and Miriam who preferred to read than be outside. They had traveled so far on boats and trains and carriages only to trap themselves in these tiny, dark rooms. Then Addie thought of Uncle Chaim and his stories about men and women traveling for hundreds of miles on the railroad, looking for work or adventure or prairies to split open with steel ploughs. He spoke of them with such hunger and delight. Oh, how she missed Uncle Chaim!

"Addie, put on my overcoat and hat and stay close to Moshe. You're tall enough that people will think you're another young man," Papa instructed. "Perhaps I should go instead."

"No, Josef," Mama said. "Moshe'll keep Addie safe. You haven't been well and Dr. Goldstein's is not very far...only the way is hard to find at night."

14

Miriam silently glided in and out of the kitchen clearing dishes. Uncle Ehud sat down next to Sammy and patted his back softly. Holding her breath, barely able to wait, Addie was afraid that Papa would change his mind if she showed her eagerness. She'd never left their apartment after sunset before.

"Go on then, Moshe, Addie. David needs the doctor."

Mama took Papa's heavy black overcoat and gray derby from the coat hook. She held out one sleeve of the coat and Addie stretched her arm deep into the soft heaviness, then her other arm into the other sleeve. The coat felt like a great, woolly blanket and so heavy that Addie pressed her knees all the way back to keep her legs from buckling. Mama placed the derby on her head. The silky inside of the brim tickled her forehead. The hat fell below her eyes, so she tipped her head and balanced it further back. The coat sleeves fell below her hands. Mama buttoned her up and kissed her forehead, saying, "You look like a small *geschäftsmann*, a businessman. Stand up tall and no one will bother you. Now hurry!"

"Go on now," Papa urged.

Four

THEY LEFT the apartment and climbed down the stairs. Addie couldn't move at her usual pace under the heavy coat and slippery derby, so Moshe was able to keep up easily and not feel badly about his leg. He didn't speak to Addie, and she thought he must be angry or embarrassed about not finding the doctor.

As they stepped outside, Addie immediately noticed the different sounds of the city at night. Piano music tinkled from several streets away and a group of men laughed somewhere in the distance. She stood up tall to keep Papa's coat from brushing against the filthy sidewalk. Moshe stayed close, though he didn't speak. Addie didn't mind. She wanted to see how the streets looked at night and to keep an eye out for Uncle Chaim. Perhaps he was one of the laughing men down the street.

They turned into the bakery alley and were suddenly thrust into pitch black. Addie reached out for Moshe's arm and almost tripped on a cobblestone. He let her hold onto him but remained silent. Her eyes began to adjust to the darkness and she could see a streetlight on Clinton Street up ahead. A scratching noise came from behind a stack of wooden crates. Addie shuddered. Uncle Chaim had told her stories about rats the size of pigs living on the streets of Chicago. He teased that the rats liked to feed on young children who strayed from home. Addie had giggled at him, back in the apartment, but now the story sent shivers through her. She let go of Moshe's arm in order to walk faster.

"Do you think David'll be all right?" she asked loudly, wanting to distract herself from the scratching noise with the sound of her voice.

Moshe grunted.

"Dr. Goldstein lives just around the corner," she continued. "I'm sorry you couldn't find it."

Moshe grunted again and then spoke. "Did you hear what Papa and Chaim were fighting over? Were they talking about the labor unions and the eight-hour day?"

Addie felt a flood of relief as they reached Clinton Street. Though she no longer needed the talk to ease her fear of the dark alley, she was eager to discuss Uncle Chaim. Perhaps Moshe knew why Papa was so angry.

"I heard Papa mention labor and capitalism. He told Uncle Chaim to go home to Germany. Do you think he'll go, Moshe? Do you know why Papa's so angry?"

"Workers all over the city...well, all over the country actually... are fighting for an eight-hour workday," Moshe began. "They want to work less hours and receive better wages and have threatened to stop working on the first of May, if they don't receive a shorter workday."

Addie counted on her fingers. The first of May was just over a week away.

She looked across Clinton Street to the horse stable, which was still and quiet at this hour. During the day, carriage men were there, watering and feeding their horses between trips. Addie thought of Uncle Ehud and Papa working so many hours a day at the hat shop, every day of the week except Shabbat. And they were grateful for the business that came. Was Uncle Chaim lazy?

"Why only eight hours, Moshe? Don't they like to work? Is that why Papa told Uncle Chaim to go back to Germany?"

They continued on Clinton Street and Addie led Moshe to the right. A group of men were gathered outside the tavern, their loud voices interspersed with the guffaws of a man too drunk to stand up straight. Moshe grabbed Addie around the shoulder and pulled her alongside of him.

"It's over here." She pointed and they crossed the street. Addie had been to Dr. Goldstein's house once before, when Mama's rheumatism had been particularly bad and she couldn't get out of bed for two days. She pointed to the door and Moshe knocked, then stood back a few feet from the threshold. Addie took off Papa's derby and held it behind her back with both hands. A minute passed before Mrs. Goldstein opened the door a crack and peeked out.

"If you're looking for the doctor, you'll have to wait a moment. We've just finished supper. Is it urgent?" Addie recognized Mrs. Goldstein from temple. Greta's mother had asked Mrs. Goldstein to be the treasurer for the Hebrew Ladies Benevolent Society two years earlier, so she often stood up after prayers to ask for donations of money and food. She had a long gray braid wrapped around the top of her head and lovely wide-set brown eyes. Though she seemed to be older than Mama and Papa, and even Uncle Ehud, her skin looked soft. She stood taller than Moshe and wore a long brown dress with a lacy bodice. She held her head high, like a proud stallion.

Moshe spoke. "Please, *Tante*. Our cousin's been coughing up blood and he's burning with fever. Our father and uncle sent us."

"Come in, then." Mrs. Goldstein sighed. "This way."

She led them into a small, brightly lit parlor. "Wait here while I get the doctor." She paused. "I pray that your cousin gets better soon." Mrs. Goldstein didn't stand quite as tall as she left the room and Addie guessed that their arrival had made her feel tired and worn down.

A daguerreotype of a fat man's profile hung above one of the sofas.

Moshe whispered, "I think she had family money from the old country to furnish this place. You know the doctor makes a pittance from his patients here."

How did Moshe come to know so much about people? Was it because he was almost a man or the eldest or just very smart? Addie nodded and eyed the delicate brocade on one of the straight-backed chairs.

Dr. Goldstein walked into the parlor with a cloth napkin tucked into his shirt. "Hello, children," he said. He wore black, square spectacles and had a well-kept mustache, thick and pointy at the ends. He was dressed handsomely, in navy trousers and a lovely silk shirt. "Mrs. Goldstein tells me your cousin's ill. Is it one of Ehud's boys?"

Moshe explained David's symptoms while the doctor listened and then nodded.

"I'll give you some medicine to take back with you and then I'll visit in the morning. Tell your parents and Ehud not to worry too much. The pills should keep him quiet overnight."

The doctor left the room for a few minutes and then returned with a brown packet wrapped in twine. "Here you are, son." He handed the packet to Moshe. "I've written instructions on the back and promise to call in the morning." Papa would surely be angry when they returned without the doctor. But Addie didn't have the courage to speak and let Moshe do the talking.

"*Danke schoen*, Doctor. Thank you. Good night."

They walked out into the night. Addie remembered the dark bakery alley and quickly calculated another route home. Closing her eyes and imagining the red line that would lead them home, she saw that they could turn on Desplaines Street from Adams, then back down to their apartment on Quincy. She took Moshe's arm and hurried him along the street.

As they walked, Addie returned to the question that had been niggling at her. "But why would Uncle Chaim want to work fewer hours, when Papa says we came to this country to have more work and make money?"

Moshe remained quiet for a moment, as if trying to find the right words to explain something difficult.

"Uncle Chaim and the others know they need to work, but the labor is terribly hard and the hours very long. It's not like sitting in the hat shop and talking and measuring heads all day. And they want to be paid the same amount for working fewer hours."

Addie had always pictured Uncle Chaim and his friends riding the trains at work or watching a parade of passengers all day. *What does it even mean to work for the railway?* she wondered.

"The railway owners would work the men to death, if they could, just to make more money. The union leaders and anarchists say the companies are riding the backs of immigrants who don't know any better and have no choice." Moshe began speaking quickly, rattling off dates and the names of all the people who'd been killed during the workers' strikes.

Addie struggled to follow and to understand what he was saying. She sucked in her breath and wrapped her arms around herself, contemplating people dying over this union business. No wonder Papa was upset. Addie thought of the railway owners and their greed and the immigrants in Chicago. She'd seen them all—the wealthy men riding in glossy black carriages, wearing fur-lined coats and pin-striped trousers and swinging gold pocket watches. The immigrants, who looked confused and forsaken, trying to understand a foreign country and a new city, struggling to find enough bread to fill the hungry mouths of their children. Addie desperately wanted to find Uncle Chaim and talk about all of these ideas with him.

As they approached the apartment, Addie thought of David and Sammy. *At least their Papa can feed them and buy medicine from the doctor.* Their home was cramped but warm enough in the winter. *Where do I fit into this great city of grit and gold, illness and adventure?* Addie longed to sit with Mama in the kitchen and tell her about the streets at night and about the labor unions stirring. But she must be careful how much she shared with Mama now, or she might not be allowed to venture into the streets at all. Suddenly, thunderous shouting pulled Addie from her thoughts.

Five

ADDIE BRACED herself against a wooden post and Moshe looked like a frightened mouse, frozen in his tracks and ears pricked up in alarm. The shouting grew louder and more rhythmic, the voices heading towards them from the west.

"Quick!" whispered Moshe, as he grabbed the end of Papa's coat sleeve and pulled Addie under a dark canvas awning. They leaned against the brick building and stood perfectly still.

The shouting bloomed into a chorus of chanting a few hundred feet away. "Eight hours of work, eight hours of rest, eight hours of what we will!"

A group of about twenty men carried large torches in the middle of the street, flames licking the night. They crossed Halsted and headed toward Addie and Moshe's hiding spot. Addie reached for Moshe's hand and held on. His hand felt warm and familiar, though she wished she hadn't grabbed for him like a baby. Down the block a number of shuttered windows opened and neighbors leaned out above the street to see what was happening.

"Quiet down!" shouted one woman from a fourth-story window across the street. Addie didn't recognize her, though she knew most of their neighbors. The woman continued to yell at the crowd below her but the chanting drowned out her voice.

"Eight hours of work, eight hours of rest, eight hours of what we will!"

Three police officers on horseback followed the crowd, clubs held high in their hands. They wore matching navy blue bowler hats. Addie winced as one smashed a man's arm with his club. The man buckled, then stood up and continued to limp along with the crowd. Moshe squeezed her hand. *He must be afraid, too.* Addie closed her eyes and imagined what the blow might feel like on her own arm—stinginess and red pulsing from the welt, and the bright, hot shame of being hit in front of friends.

A man several stories above the awning called out to the police officers from his window. "What have these men done? Let them be."

Several other neighbors began talking loudly to one another across their open windows.

"Eight hours of work, eight hours of rest, eight hours of what we will!" the men kept shouting.

Addie thought about those words strung together, chanted with so much passion by grown men. She counted in her head. *How many hours do I sit at my desk at school? Seven. And how many hours do I sleep at night? Nine. And what does it mean, "eight hours of what we will"?* She looked at her ten fingers. *What is it that I will? What is it that I want?* She wanted to fly along the streets like a sparrow, flying from here to there with no tether. She wanted Uncle Chaim to come back and Papa to greet him with an embrace. She wanted David to stop coughing and return to the merry boy who made her laugh.

Some people cheered and began clapping from their windows. Others called to the men to go home or quiet down. The police didn't seem to notice the neighbors' words and continued to hustle the men along with their horses and clubs. Two of the police officers straddled each flank of the crowd, the third herded them from behind. Addie held her breath and closed her eyes, praying that it would be over soon.

Just then, the front door of their apartment building rattled. Someone was coming out to the street. Addie opened her eyes. There, on the bottom step, stood Papa, panting. Beads of sweat dotted his temples. His eyes darted about the street as he searched the crowd. He must have come looking for them when he heard the racket on the street.

Moshe held his finger to his lips and Addie understood that he wanted to remain hidden from Papa. She longed to run to Papa and reassure him. *Why does Moshe want to keep Papa from seeing us? Perhaps he doesn't want Papa to know we've seen the crowd of shouting men.* It would be better for Papa to believe they were still with Dr. Goldstein or on their way home. *Will I ever be as clever as Moshe and understand the world of grown-ups?*

The streetlight lit up the left side of Papa's face, just a few feet away from where they stood. Addie rarely saw Papa away from the apartment, or outside the hat shop, and was curious if his face looked different when he was alone. Suddenly his features contorted, his upper lip curled into a snarl, his long brow furrowed and his cheeks and chin lurched forward as though preparing to attack. His eyes fixed on a point in the crowd. Addie turned to see what Papa was looking at. She craned her neck and moved her head to catch a better view as the group passed. The chanting vibrated through her body.

"Eight hours of work, eight hours of rest, eight hours of what we will."

Addie caught her breath. There, in the middle of the crowd, was Uncle Chaim. He was working his way toward the front and seemed to be trying to talk to one of the leaders, who was holding a torch. Moshe sucked in his breath. He must have seen Uncle Chaim, too. Addie stared at her uncle, utterly fascinated. *What is he doing walking with all these men? Is this the union Papa spoke of?* Uncle Chaim looked serious and worried, not at all like her playful companion. He was tall compared to the other men, with his broad shoulders and erect posture. *Did he leave our apartment to join these men? Or did he just happen to meet the group as they paraded through the streets? Are those his friends from the railway?* If only Addie could run out to him and ask him all these questions. He was so close, and yet as far away as the old country.

Moshe grabbed Addie's hand and pulled her along as he ran the few steps to Papa. Their father's face changed to a look of surprise and relief upon seeing them. He took one last look at the crowd and then turned back to their apartment building, grabbing Moshe by the shoulder and pushing him into the safety of the building, with Addie trailing behind. They climbed the first set of stairs in silence. The chanting faded a bit and Papa stopped on the landing to catch his breath. His shoulders sagged, as if he'd just arrived from a long voyage.

"Why did you take so long? Did you find the doctor?" Papa's anger boiled just below his relief and exhaustion. Moshe knew how to calm him down.

"Papa, we got medicine for David. Here." He pulled the packet from his pocket and handed it to their father, to take his mind off the men on the street. "Dr. Goldstein will come tomorrow morning to see David." Moshe gritted his teeth and paused. He seemed to be in pain. "We saw those men just as we came around the last corner and hid under the awning until they passed. I shielded Addie so that she'd be safe."

Papa studied Moshe in the dim light of the stairway, then looked at Addie. It felt as if his eyes were boring under her skin and she desperately wanted to race up the steps away from him.

"Were you frightened by the men? Are you all right?" He sounded more angry than concerned. Maybe he wanted to know if they'd seen Uncle Chaim. Addie felt her stomach somersault and her heart quicken. She stayed silent and prayed that Moshe would respond.

"Yes, Papa. We're fine. Addie knew the way to the doctor and we're home safe now." Moshe seemed nervous and turned to climb the next set of stairs. "How's David?" he asked.

"He's still feverish, but he's stopped coughing up blood," Papa responded.

With the subject changed to David, Addie breathed deeply into her belly. They walked the remaining stairs in silence and Addie's mind returned to Uncle Chaim, marching amidst the men in the street.

Six

ADDIE CLIMBED into bed and settled under the scratchy gray blanket next to Miriam. Trying to lie still, she   rotated her left foot around and around while her mind whirled. She turned onto her right side, away from Miriam, and folded her knees into her chest. *What was Uncle Chaim doing in the crowd of angry men? Is he in danger?*

Addie wanted to warn Mama about Uncle Chaim. But Mama was taking care of David now, and she didn't want to disturb Miriam by getting up. The medicine from Dr. Goldstein had quieted David's cough, and Mama was humming him a tune from the old country. Addie wished she could be the one sitting on Mama's lap right now. The tune made her drowsy.

Guten Abend, gute Nacht,
mit Rosen bedacht,
mit Näglein besteckt,

Good evening, good night,
With roses covered,
With carnations adorned...

She rolled onto her back, careful not to pull the blanket from Miriam's thin body, and stretched out her long torso and legs. With her eyes closed, she saw Papa's face again—framed by the apartment door, as it had been less than an hour ago—with dark eyes, beady and menacing.

schlupf unter die Deck!
Morgen früh, wenn Gott will,
wirst du wieder geweckt.

Slip under the covers.
Tomorrow morning, if God wants so,
you will wake once again.

Addie desperately hoped that God would want David to wake up in the morning. *Does God have a will, too?* Her fingers gripped the edge of the blanket as she drifted into a fitful sleep, aware of Miriam's steady breathing all through the night.

⌒

"Boys and girls," Miss Green called, "please complete page nine in your primers."

Addie's skin itched in the thick air of the classroom and the words in her book swam around the page. The girl who shared her desk, Frances Jamieson, smelled of molasses and picked her nose when she thought no one was looking. Addie shifted in her seat and adjusted her legs under the cramped desk every few minutes. Greta, who sat exactly two rows ahead of Addie, wore her blonde hair in tight little curls that were tied up every night by her mother. Greta was small and slender with a round, pink-cheeked doll's face. Addie watched her head bob up and down as she copied math problems from the chalkboard into her book and wished she would turn around so they could try to read each other's minds.

Ever since Mrs. Raczynski had taken them to see a spirit medium, Madame Devereux—who could speak to the dead and read peoples' minds—Addie and Greta had tried to send each other silent messages during class. Madame Devereux had told a boy in the front row of the audience that he shouldn't sneak a frog into his grandmother's bed, which caused the boy to run out of the tent looking white as a sheet of fresh paper. Papa would never have allowed Addie to go the medium, but Mrs. Raczynski said that sometimes it was better to beg for forgiveness than to ask for permission. Luckily, Mama and Papa had never asked where she'd gone that day. Addie still wasn't sure if she wanted to tell Greta about Uncle Chaim, so maybe it was better if Greta didn't turn around and try to read her mind.

Addie loved Mrs. Raczynski. She was sturdy like an oak tree and was a woman of the world, but she treated Addie like she would any adult. She spent her afternoons going door to door for the Hebrew Ladies Benevolent Society, bringing the poor families of Chicago food and blankets and medicine. Addie wished she could go with her, peeking into homes and busying herself with important tasks, but she usually had to stay and tend the hat shop. Instead, Greta—who was more interested in the latest fashion magazines and drawing stick pictures of the boys in class—got to see all the neighborhoods of Chicago and to help her mother.

Just before noon Miss Green, who wore her graying hair in a tight bun near the top of her head, stopped in front of Addie's desk. Some of the children called her "Pincushion" in the schoolyard, but Addie liked her and preferred not to tease.

"Are you ill, Addie? You don't look well today."

Blushing, Addie sat up straight.

"No, ma'am. I'm fine."

"I understand the Knights of Labor marched in the neighborhood last night. Did they keep you up?"

Addie's mind raced. *Perhaps Miss Green can help me make sense of last night.* If only she could think of the right questions to ask, without letting on that Uncle Chaim was involved.

Before Addie could think of a response, Miss Green said, "My three younger brothers joined the Knights. I worry for their safety but something must be done about the working conditions in the factories and stockyards."

Addie narrowed her eyes in concentration, trying to work out what Miss Green had just said. *Why'd she tell me about her brothers? Isn't she ashamed to have family involved in the union?*

Miss Green placed her hand on Addie's shoulder. "Addie, are you sure you're all right? You look unwell. Why don't you stay home after the noon meal and rest this afternoon?"

Addie nodded but still couldn't form words. Miss Green looked at her for another moment and then nodded curtly, as though she'd made a decision. The back of her pleated skirt swished from side to side as she walked to the front of the classroom.

"Girls and boys." Miss Green rapped a ruler on her desk. The fourteen students placed their pencils down and looked up.

"Some of you may have heard men protesting in the streets last night." Addie's stomach tightened. Greta turned around in her seat and widened her eyes at Addie in excitement. "Your parents may or may not have discussed this with you, but I feel I must tell you that these men are angry with the large companies that work them to the bone. They're not angry at you and your families. But do be careful. The parades could turn violent."

Josephine McCarthy, a tiny girl who'd joined the class only the week before, gasped dramatically and two boys shot up their hands.

"Thomas, please stand and state your question," Miss Green said.

The older of the two boys stood up and cleared his throat. "Miss Green, my dad says that the police have attacked the protesters with clubs and sticks, but I thought the police are supposed to protect us." Addie could tell that Thomas's parents were Americans by his thick Chicago accent and his trust in the police. Most immigrants didn't think the police were supposed to help or protect them.

James McKenna, a red-haired boy with an ugly scar across his chin, and Bernie Alexander, the smartest boy in the class, whispered to each other in the back row. The rest waited for Miss Green to respond.

"Oh, children. These are difficult times." She looked out the window and furrowed her brow. She spoke slowly and deliberately, as though picking each word out of boiling water.

"The police work for the city government to protect people and keep order in Chicago. But sometimes things are not completely clear." She walked back to her desk.

Alfred, the other boy with his hand raised, coughed quietly to attract Miss Green's attention. Addie knew Alfred's family from temple. His older sister had a withered leg and leaned into her father as they walked side by side along the streets. She and Addie were in the same Sunday school class and had helped each other memorize their Hebrew prayers. Miss Green nodded at Alfred. He was very shy, the youngest in a large family, and Addie was curious to hear what question burned him enough to speak up in front of the whole class.

"Ma'am." His voice was barely a squeak. "Why do the working men march at night?" Alfred sat down quickly and placed his hands on his cheeks as if to cool them.

Miss Green sat down in her chair and suddenly looked very tired. The room stood still. Addie prayed that Miss Green would explain it all to them, so she wouldn't have to wonder anymore.

"While that's an excellent question, Alfred, I think it's best for each of your parents to answer it for you," Miss Green finally said. "Class is dismissed." Addie's heart sank. She lingered at her desk in case Miss Green decided to say more.

Meanwhile, Greta had pushed her way to Addie's desk. "Mama told me to rush home after morning lessons so that I can help her cook for some of the union families who are planning to strike soon. Will you come?"

Addie felt torn. "Miss Green told me to go home and rest. She says I don't look well."

"Well, schmell," Greta sang. "Come on! Mama's cooking latkes and we need your help."

Suddenly, Addie felt a dense heaviness in her chest and back. She wanted to be alone so that she could think. "No, you go on," she said and in her mind she begged Greta to stop asking her. Greta's face changed, became serious, and Addie wondered if there was something to this mind reading business.

"Okay, then. See you later." And Greta was off just like that, without a care in the world.

Addie walked home in a daze and climbed up the steps of their building with a terrible sense of dread. If Mama had no errands for her to run she'd be stuck in the apartment until tomorrow morning. *I must be good and work on my quilt and learn to sit still, as Miriam does.* Mama had saved scraps of calico and striped cloth for Addie to sew into her first patchwork. When she opened the apartment door David was lying asleep on the sofa. She tiptoed into the kitchen where Mama was shucking peas and boiling water.

"Mama, Miss Green says I look ill and should stay home today. But I feel all right, only a bit frightened by the group of men Moshe and I saw on the street last night, and the police on horses chasing them with sticks." The words poured out in the warm kitchen. She paused and watched for her mother's reaction. Mama's lips pursed and her face narrowed with concern.

"You're talking about the men on the street last night?"

Addie nodded.

"Yes, we heard them, too. . .just before you and Moshe returned from Dr. Goldstein's."

Addie waited for more.

"Papa will want you at home when you're not at school or the shop and you must obey him. The streets are not safe for you children."

Addie mustered up her courage. "Mama, tell me more about the Knights of Labor and about Uncle Chaim."

"Hush, child," Mama said, cutting her off. She spoke gently but without any room for compromise. "Those are the affairs of adults. Go sit quietly and work your quilt and I'll bring you some chamomile tea and bread."

Addie waited another moment, hoping that Mama might change her mind and say something about Uncle Chaim. Finally, resigned to her mother's silence, she slunk out of the kitchen, shoulders hunched down and chin tucked into her chest. She pulled out two pieces of fabric. One was so frayed that it couldn't be sewn onto the whole without building a new edge. She sighed heavily at the tedious work ahead.

Seven

I WILL *NOT* stand for it!" Papa cried out. Addie woke with a start to the sound of raised voices. "He only just came to America and already he's causing trouble. We've been here for years, working to create lives for ourselves. While I'm busy feeding my children and running my business, he runs around with communists and anarchists and then sleeps on my couch at night." Papa slammed his fist against the table. "Thousands of workers plan to take to the streets this very weekend, which will shut the city down and push our business under the ground!"

Late afternoon shadows lay across Addie's bed. Mama had sent her to rest and the apartment had been so quiet then, with all the family out but Mama and David. Someone had moved David to Moshe's cot where he was asleep now. Papa's voice sounded like a thunderstorm raging in the front room.

"Josef, Josef. Calm yourself. There are many good men joining the unions. Perhaps Chaim just happened upon the parade after he left our house on Shabbat."

Addie's ears perked up. She swallowed hard and listened.

Papa stomped about the front room, his footfalls heavy against the wooden floor. "It was no accident that he was there. You must know that, Sara! He joined the Knights and now may be consorting with anarchists who are calling for violence towards the very companies that employ them! And Addie and Moshe...they may have seen him for all we know...out in the streets, causing chaos."

How could Uncle Chaim be part of a union when Papa thinks they're so bad? Isn't it the unions that are causing all the problems in Chicago? Turning over and hiding her head under the quilt, Addie wished desperately that the shouting would stop. Her head began to spin like the bright purple top Uncle Ehud had given the boys at the new year. *Perhaps I should go into the front room. Maybe they'll stop arguing if they see me.*

"No harm's been done," Mama repeated, sounding almost desperate now. "Surely Chaim isn't too deeply involved in the Knights if he's only just joined." Mama's voice stopped short. She sounded as though she had more to say. *Perhaps she remembers how close David and I are and is just now holding her index finger to her pursed lips to show Papa that they must stop their quarreling.* Addie struggled to sit up in bed but then felt as though her head was filled with wet sand, so lay back down.

"I tell you this, Sara," Papa continued, though his voice was lower now. "The union activity's bound to end in more violence and then people will stop going out, or they'll leave the city altogether and the shop will close, along with so many other businesses. And then what? We'll all go work for the packinghouses like the other Germans?" His voice grew louder. "We came here to escape politics and poverty and now they're upon us again—like feral dogs."

A snarling wolf appeared in Addie's mind, with teeth bared and saliva flying. The animal's paws were upon Papa's shoulders so that it stood as tall as he—eye to eye—and threatened to bite his neck. Addie shook her head and opened her eyes.

"Mama!" she burst out, for the wolf felt close and her throat burned. "Mama!"

"Josef, you must stay calm." Mama kept talking. She hadn't heard Addie. "Chaim has his friends with the railway, perhaps some of them are involved with the anarchists. But he wants no trouble for our family, only fair wages." Mama stretched her words out slowly and carefully, trying to soothe Papa now. The warmth of her voice made Addie sleepy.

33

"Anyway," she continued, "most people can't just leave the city. They have work here, and their families, and have no other places to go. Think of the trouble in Berlin. And yet the city was always full of people. You must also realize, Josef, that men will always need your hats to wear, to cover their heads and parade about like so many roosters."

Suddenly Papa chuckled. A spell had been broken. Addie's legs and arms grew warm and heavy as Papa sighed and began to laugh.

"Oh, Sara, your grand philosophies about men and their hats." Papa chuckled again. "Tell me more."

A chair scraped against the floor and Addie guessed that Mama had moved to sit closer to Papa.

"You think after all these years of being the wife and sister-in-law of hat sellers I have noticed nothing?" She sounded much younger, teasing and flirting, with all the time in the world and no thought of getting the next meal ready.

"Do tell me, Sara." Papa's voice sounded low and sweet, and Addie's face flushed red. She felt ashamed for eavesdropping.

"Well," Mama began, sounding pleased with herself. "The aristocrats want hats all of their own, to signal to each other their wealth and taste, like the top hat, for example. For some time, the new hat of the day will be in the clutches of only the richest of men who can afford the material and careful design of the most expert hat makers."

It sounded like Mama was telling Papa a bedtime story. Addie rolled over and snuggled down in the quilts, relishing Mama's story and the way Papa loved hearing her talk.

Mama continued. "But, by and by, the new hat will be seen on the street being worn by all manner of men—the cooper, the baker and liveryman, even the factory worker. There is nothing that dictates *which* hat a man can wear, so long as he covers his head while outside."

Mama paused, waiting to see if Papa would respond. When he didn't, she concluded, "And so you see, Josef, your line of work is secure, as the rich man will always want the latest fashions, to prove his place in society, and the poor man will always need your hats, to prove that he still has his pride. Your business is as tried and true as that of the tax collector!"

"Bah!" Papa responded. "Now you compare me to a tax collector!" He sounded amused but the edge had returned to his voice and the lovely talking was over.

Mama changed the subject before Papa could begin to rant about the anarchists again.

"Josef, I didn't have a chance to tell you. Addie is home from school. She's exhausted and seems a bit ill."

Papa sounded surprised. "She's home now?" His heavy footsteps thudded down the corridor and Addie quickly pulled the quilt over her face. The door opened and she could imagine his eyes boring into her. He shut the door and spoke quietly to Mama.

Addie moved the quilt down again and stared at the dark ceiling. She thought of the rich men with silken top hats and then remembered a drawing of President Abraham Lincoln in her primer. He was the one who'd freed the slaves in the Civil War and wore the hat called the stovepipe. He'd been a poor boy from the woods of Kentucky and Illinois and then became president of the United States. *Did he become president by wearing the hat of rich men, or did he only wear the hat once he'd become a senator from Illinois? And why doesn't Papa wear a top hat, if he's so keen on being rich?*

Eight

ONLY THE richest families in Chicago could afford to live along the shores of Lake Michigan. Cherry-cheeked children in sailor suits stretched their legs along the grassy shores of the great lake and fished and swam there in the hot summer months, or so Moshe described them after he delivered newspapers there. But Papa heard from a customer that immigrant families could enjoy the lakefront in Lincoln Park. The customer, a Russian Jew, had taken his family there several times and found the place to be like the old country. Papa often complained about the Russian Jews who, unlike the German Jews, were just getting themselves established in Chicago and didn't act enough like Americans.

Addie couldn't remember visiting the Oder River with Mama, Moshe, Miriam, and her Oma and Opa when she was a baby, but Mama told stories about their visits. They'd lived in a small town and could walk several miles from their stone house to a swimming spot on the river. Even as a baby, Addie had loved to splash in the water. She had no fear of getting wet, so Mama had to watch her carefully.

Now that David seemed a bit better, and was able to walk around the apartment without bursting into violent coughs, Papa thought the whole family should go to the park on Sunday. Uncle Ehud was tired and sad looking, and Papa said the fresh air would do them all good.

Addie guessed that Papa had other reasons for wanting them away from the center of the city. Saturday was to be the first day of the union marches. Moshe said that tens of thousands of workers would be marching along Michigan Avenue, with Albert Parsons leading the crowd. On the way home from school Moshe explained that Parsons was the founder of a group called the International Working People's Association, which demanded fair treatment of immigrants and laborers. Ten thousand workers from the Chicago lumberyards were planning to take to the streets. Addie tried to crowd ten thousand people along the maplines in her mind but her eyes got squinty and began to water.

Mama was up extra early that morning, even before the sun came up, to prepare the picnic. She hadn't been able to work the day before, as it was still the Sabbath. Addie woke to the sound of the kettle boiling and Mama humming in the kitchen, and let herself snuggle under the covers for a few more precious moments. Though she missed Uncle Chaim a great deal, David was improving and Papa and Mama had stopped looking so worried all the time. Perhaps, with less to worry about, Papa would forgive Uncle Chaim and he could return home. The union strikes would end after today and the family would be its whole self again, like she hoped her quilt would be someday.

They all ate bread around the table before preparing to leave for the day. Uncle Ehud kept his eye on David throughout breakfast but David didn't notice the extra attention and gobbled down his bread like any normal boy. Addie's chest swelled. *Our family is almost right again.* While Mama and Miriam were still eating Papa rose and said, "Come. Let's go!"

Miriam scolded him. "Papa! Let me finish my bread. You're acting like a little boy."

Mama's laugh rang out like a big bell for the first time in many weeks, maybe months. "Your father wants to be the first one at the park so he can get the nicest spot." But Addie felt almost certain that Papa wanted to get through downtown early in case there was trouble, and perhaps to avoid talk of the unions and Uncle Chaim.

With that, Mama collected the lunch pails and the rest of the family rose and left the apartment. Papa led the way with Miriam and Sammy right behind. Addie walked in the middle of the party with Uncle Ehud and David, then Moshe and Mama followed behind. Moshe always walked in the back to avoid being noticed or pitied. Addie's legs itched to race ahead and leave the others far behind, but she was hemmed in the middle of her family.

They made their way to Van Buren Street, to the stop for the horse-drawn streetcar that would take them downtown, where they would transfer to the Clark Street line. They formed a tight knot on the wooden sidewalk and waited. *Something is different today,* Addie realized. She turned around in a complete circle. *What is it?* She looked up at the blue sky and the line of buildings and houses and realized that the sky was clear today, with no smoke or haze from the factories. Normally, a dense curtain of black soot hung on the horizon but the workers were striking today so the factories were shut.

Addie hardly ever rode on the streetcars, since she rarely traveled beyond their neighborhood. A very crowded-looking car pulled up and Addie dreaded the feeling of being pressed up against strangers. Many of the passengers were young men carrying pamphlets. *They must be working men on their way to the march.* Addie lingered by the back of her family, hoping that she'd be the last one to climb aboard and could stand near a window. Papa climbed on the rickety car first and paid for the whole family out of his change purse. He counted out eleven copper coins and handed them to the driver who instructed them to pass. Addie climbed on last and stood near the door looking out a narrow window at the street, the thick smell of hard-working men and cigars assaulting her nose.

The streetcar crawled along Van Buren, picking up passengers, mostly men, every few blocks. Three men stood in a cluster at another stop, their heads close together and all talking at once with spit flying and their fists raised. Then the streetcar stopped in the crowded downtown area, where the filthy streets, splotched with piles of horse dung and heaps of burning trash, were filling up with people. Bright banners and flags decorated some of the buildings.

"The flags with stars and stripes represent the Knights of Labor and the crimson banners belong to the anarchists," Moshe whispered in Addie's ear.

The mood of the crowd seemed festive and almost carnival like, not the serious, heavy affair that Addie expected. But Papa quickly herded them to the stop for the Clark Street streetcar, anxious to get them away from the hubbub. As they traveled north the downtown gave way to pretty neighborhoods with swaybacked houses. A woman stood working in a flower bed outside a large white clapboard house. *What would it be like to live with so much open space, with green and pretty things all about?* Every once in a while, Addie caught sight of the lake peeking between the buildings. She looked out across the water and thought about the children living on the other side. *Do they have angry fathers and sick cousins and uncles who run away? Are thousands of workers gathering to march on the other side of the lake?*

Suddenly, Sammy grabbed her hand, pulling her away from faraway thoughts. "Papa says this is where we have to get off."

Addie looked up and realized that the car was nearly empty except for her family. All the other passengers had already tumbled off and were making their way into the park.

"Let's hurry so we can get a good spot for our picnic," Papa said. "I'll carry David on my shoulders if he needs help."

The grassy areas were already crowded with families picnicking. The lake sparkled blue through the trees and reflected the white, downy clouds hanging in the sky. The water looked so beautiful—dark blue and peaceful and inviting. Addie inhaled deeply through her nose, smelling fresh air with no trace of animal dung. Two young boys played chase along one of the paths. Beyond them Addie spotted a copse of friendly elm trees. The sky felt open and broad, and Addie longed to take off and fly, the way she did in her dreams.

Suddenly she realized that her family had moved far down toward an open spot closer to the lake. She wanted to keep gazing out at the trees forever but was afraid of losing sight of Mama and Papa in the mix of immigrant families who resembled her own—the whiskery, round men and stout, strong women holding onto babies and herding children. Addie kept her eyes fixed on Miriam's blue dress and picked her way through the other families. They finally settled in an open spot, where Mama spread out a blanket from her basket and began to set out the food. She carefully unpacked a round loaf of brown bread, then thick sausages and pickles and baked potatoes. Addie's stomach rumbled. Papa and Uncle Ehud ate first, then Moshe and Miriam, and finally Mama and Addie and the two little boys. The food tasted even more delicious outside—the sausage cold and tangy in her mouth, and the inside of the loaf of bread soft and chewy. Belly full, Addie stood up, ready to explore the park.

"Papa, may I go and look at the water?" she asked.

"Moshe, take the children down to the water." Sometimes Addie wished that Papa would answer her directly. Lately it seemed that he only spoke to her when he was angry or impatient.

Moshe stood up and crammed a last bite of sausage into his mouth. Sammy and David jumped up and they all walked toward the lake.

"David should not get wet!" Mama called out. Her voice sounded high and fretful.

Moshe spoke to David. "You have to stay away from the water or I'll have to bring you back to the blanket. Okay?"

David nodded.

Bigger children played in the water and a few men in bathing costumes swam farther out into the surf. The waves were only a few feet high, but Addie stayed away from the water's edge. Moshe took off his shoes and rolled up the cuffs of his trousers to wade in the shallows.

"Stay back with Addie, David," Moshe called.

Sammy copied Moshe and took off his shoes and rolled up his trousers. Addie took David's hand and squeezed, knowing how much he wanted to play in the water because she felt the same way. Her stockings itched but Papa would shout if she took them off and dipped her feet in the lovely blue water. Of course she didn't know how to swim but the thought of the cool water on her feet was tempting. She felt restless and, though she knew Moshe shouldn't walk more, she couldn't help herself.

"Let's go to those trees and get a better look at the lake," she called out.

They walked along the lake, past several groups of men and boys wading in the water. Almost all of the women and girls stayed back on their blankets with the food and the babies. Addie felt a pang of guilt for not helping Mama clean up the meal but she knew that Miriam enjoyed fussing over food. She pushed away the guilt and looked out over the glittering expanse of water. They walked for about ten minutes, past more clusters of bathers.

"It's so beautiful!" Addie exclaimed. "I wish we could come here every week."

"Back in Germany, we'd go to the river every week and play for hours in the water," Moshe said. "We'd pick fresh plums and pears from the trees and walk for miles through the countryside. Miriam and I would climb trees and Papa'd play hide and seek with us."

Addie could hardly believe her ears. *Papa used to play? Miriam was allowed to climb trees?* Addie knew they'd visited the river and trees and open space, but now the thought of it made her stomach squirm. Mama and Papa and Moshe and Miriam had lived an entire lifetime before her. Surely she'd missed out on the most wonderful golden years her family had spent together. Germany

41

shimmered in front of her, like a dream just beyond the reach of her memory.

Moshe sensed her sadness and jealousy. "Oh, Addie. There were many problems in the old country, as well. America's a good place to be. Our family will prosper here."

I'm not so sure, Addie thought. She wanted to ask Moshe more about the union marches but decided not to, since the twins were in earshot.

"Let's walk back to the others," Moshe said, changing the subject.

When they returned to the blanket Addie sat down next to Mama. Papa and Uncle Ehud and Miriam had spotted their neighbors the Swarztmans on a blanket close by, and had gone to say hello. Moshe, David, and Sammy wandered back to the water. Mama was sitting up with her eyes closed.

Addie pressed her fingers into the cool grass and heard two men speaking on a nearby blanket.

"Now the company says they don't have enough work for me or my brother, so we'll not be able to afford the debt on our apartment," one said to the other. Addie wanted to turn around to see their faces, but was afraid they'd stop talking if they knew she could hear them.

"We're in the same boat. They tell us to come in by five o'clock in the morning and then send us away with no work. They have us wrapped about their fingers. We'd be at the march today, only my wife insists that it's too dangerous, that the police and the companies will do anything to keep us down."

"Yes, us, too. My brother's there. He was told he must work twelve hour shifts day in and day out or he'll lose his place at the stockyards," continued the first.

"You won't see him or his family here enjoying themselves and letting their children get some fresh air."

The second man clucked his tongue.

"Such a shame. People need time away from the city and

packinghouses. What's the point of life otherwise, if there's no time to enjoy God's creation?"

Mama's eyes opened and Addie realized she was still eavesdropping and should ignore the men's conversation.

"Oh, Mama, the water is so beautiful here! It's so clear and fresh."

Mama smiled and nodded.

"Is it true that Papa played with Miriam and Moshe along the rivers, and they climbed trees and picked plums and pears?" The words tumbled out before Addie could consider how they would make Mama feel.

Mama's smile tightened. "I took you to the river, too, Addie... after Papa came to America. It's only that you were too young to remember. But the river and trees and air live inside of you from those days, even if you don't have the memories in your head." Mama stared far out into the water, as though trying to remember something important.

"Mama, what do you miss most about the old country?"

Mama turned to Addie with her brow furrowed in concentration. She spoke slowly. "I try not to think of it too often. It would be too difficult to make the journey again, even if just for a visit, and now, truly, America is our home."

She went silent and Addie felt deflated by her answer. But then she continued, "I do miss the countryside...and what I miss most of all is my vegetable garden. We had a small plot on the side of the house and I grew potatoes and turnips and flowers and garden peas and onions." She looked back at the lake. "I miss the smell of the earth on my fingers."

Addie felt another pang of homesickness, though for a place and time she couldn't even remember.

"Mama," Addie ventured, daring herself to ask a question that had gnawed at her for years. "Does Papa love me?"

Clasping Addie's hand, Mama smiled. "Oh, Addie, you are our *schatzi*, our little treasure. The icing on our cake. But Papa didn't know you as a baby and only met you when you were four years old and we came to Chicago. It took him time to get to know you, to see himself in you. But, yes, he loves you, Addie. As much as he loves Moshe and Miriam, only the love looks a little different." She used her kind-sad voice. Addie looked away and felt some relief. *But the love looks a little different.*

Soon the others returned and Mama began to pack everything up. She folded the blanket back into its neat square. Other families began to pack up their belongings and the sight made Addie's throat feel tight and achy. She liked seeing so many people together, enjoying themselves. Everyone on the streets of Chicago moved so quickly to get somewhere fast. The people in their neighborhood rarely smiled and seemed pressed down by an invisible hand. They retraced their steps, back to where they could catch the streetcar that would take them home. The air suddenly felt cool and Addie shivered against the coming night.

Nine

HEY WON'T stop this nonsense! Now the workers are
striking at the McCormick Reaper Works," Papa roared.
He slammed the newspaper on the table and stormed
down the hallway to Mama, who was folding clothes in the back
bedroom. Staring down at her primer and staying perfectly still
at the table, Addie waited for Mama to respond.

"Addie, run to the shop and fetch a pound of white flour so
I can make a cake for dinner," Mama called from down the hall.
Addie stood up slowly, reluctant to leave, and stole a quick glance
at the front page of the newspaper.

She blazed down the apartment steps two at a time and
found a group of children playing hopscotch on the sidewalk.
For a moment she considered joining them. Her pulse quickened.
No time to play today. Windows on the lower floors of apartments
were shuttered, as though the city was hiding out during the
worker strikes. Crossing Desplaines Street, Addie cut over to the
north corner of the block and headed toward the store. Passing
by the park, she noticed a young couple standing together under
an elm tree. They faced each other and clasped hands, holding
perfectly still, as though caught in a photograph. The young man
wore a beige peaked cap that was crisp and new looking. The girl
was much shorter than him, almost a foot it seemed, and strained
her head up to look into the young man's eyes. Suddenly Addie
recognized the girl's hat and realized it was Miriam. She stopped in

her tracks, took several steps back, then wheeled around and ran straight into the bosom of a stout woman ambling up the street.

"Watch out, girl!" the woman cried.

Addie was terrified that the woman's shout would catch Miriam's attention. Mumbling an apology, she looked down at the sidewalk and walked as quickly as she could to the next street. Once safely out of sight, she stopped and peered back around the corner. *Who is that boy? And why on earth is Miriam holding hands with him?* Addie didn't recognize him from school or temple, though she could only make out his profile and the cap covering his head. He was tall and lean, and seemed mesmerized by Miriam. Miriam pulled away from him and they began to walk along the street. Addie's mind spun and whirled like the inside of Papa's pocket watch. *Does Mama know about this boy? Surely Papa doesn't know or he'd be angry with Miriam.* While Papa had no patience for Addie, he loved to gently tease Miriam about how fast she read her books and how slowly she picked though her meals. *Surely he doesn't know about this boy!*

Addie continued on to the store, barely seeing anything around her as she considered what it meant for Miriam to be holding hands with a young man. *Is he an immigrant, as well, or an American?* Addie shuddered to think of Papa's reaction to Miriam seeing a strange boy unknown to the family. *He might not even be Jewish.* Addie reached the store and pushed all of her weight against the heavy wooden door to make it swing open. Bells jingled. Once inside she walked straight to the counter to place her order.

Addie loved the general store, with bolts of bright cotton and silk patterns and barrels of cider and high shelves filled with boxes and jars of metal screws and tallow candles and twine. The store was at least three times larger than the hat shop, and Addie relished the feeling of space in it. Papa and Uncle Ehud always greeted customers as they walked into the hat shop and asked what they were looking for, but the owner of the general store let his customers look around for as long as they liked, without questions.

Today, however, Addie didn't want to wander around the store. She couldn't blot the image of Miriam and the young man from her mind. An elderly man, shriveled and with white whiskers covering his cheeks and chin, stood at the front of the counter holding a long list in front of him. He squinted at the paper and barked out items to the storekeeper, who stood behind the counter. The storekeeper wore a crisp apron tied about his narrow waist and a starched white shirt, with a bowtie and red suspenders.

"Two pounds of white sugar—Cuban, if you happen to have it."

"Certainly," the storekeeper sang out in a friendly way. He glided behind the counter to the shelves as though on ice skates. He began scooping sugar from a large tin into a hemp sack.

Addie's mind wandered. *How is it that Miriam's so good around Mama and Papa, and studying to be a teacher, while also seeing a strange young man in the park?* Her thoughts were interrupted by the sound of bells at the door and Greta's high voice.

"Addie!" Greta cried out and ran over to her friend.

Addie tried to smile and hide her worry, but Greta could tell that something was wrong.

"What is it?" she whispered, looking both worried and conspiratorial. "Quick, tell me before Mama comes in."

Addie eyed the shop door, hoping that Mrs. Raczynski would come in and save her from deciding whether or not to tell Greta about Miriam. She sighed, feeling disloyal to Miriam but also desperate for companionship in her secret. "It's Miriam," she said. "I saw her just now in the park with a boy...holding hands...a boy I've never seen before."

Greta gasped in shock, but the corners of her mouth were turned up ever so slightly and her eyes twinkled. Addie regretted telling and felt even more alone. Before Greta could ask any more questions, Mrs. Raczynski came into the store and walked over to the girls. "Hello, Addie! How are you today?"

Addie looked down and forced a smile. "Fine, thank you, ma'am."

"Are you here for your mama?" Mrs. Raczynski asked.

"Yes. I'm buying flour for her to make a cake." Addie felt shy, in spite of Mrs. Raczynski's warmth and interest in her.

"Mama," Greta interjected. "Can Addie come with us today? Please!" Greta grabbed Addie's hands and squeezed. "It'll be so much less boring for me if Addie can come, too." She turned to Addie. "We're bringing food to the families of the men striking... all afternoon, down in Packingtown, where the meatpackers live. It's so hot and tiresome and I want you to come and keep me company. Please, Mama?" Her voice sounded fierce-high.

Addie felt torn inside. She should get home with the flour *and* she still hoped to find out more about Uncle Chaim *and* she needed to sort out her thoughts about Miriam and the boy. But, if she went to Packingtown and met the families of the striking men, maybe she could find out something about Uncle Chaim. Curiosity about the area around the stockyards, where the poorest immigrants lived and worked, gnawed at her. She knew that the stockyards were made up of thousands of pens, which held hogs and cows and other animals, with the meatpacking buildings scattered throughout. The animals were slaughtered and butchered, and then the meat was transported by rail all over America. Hundreds of immigrants moved to the area every day looking for work in the slaughterhouses.

And she wanted to help. To be sturdy and proud and useful like Mrs. Raczynski. But Papa would never allow her to go there, even with the Hebrew Ladies Benevolent Society. She wrung her hands behind her back. Mrs. Raczynski studied her closely and, as though reading her mind, put her out of her misery.

"Not today, Greta. We'll be out well past dark and I wouldn't ask that of Addie and her family. It's miles from here and it'll take us hours to get there and back."

As Greta began to protest, the line moved forward and it was Addie's turn to order. The shop owner smiled at her. "And how are your Papa and Ehud faring these days? Keeping the heads of men well covered, I hope?" he asked, with a chuckle.

"Yes, sir," Addie answered shyly.

The shop owner brought Addie the flour, made a mark in his notebook, and moved on to Mrs. Raczynski.

Greta eyed a golden locket in the glass cabinet near the front counter. "Please, Mama! My birthday's next month and I promise not to ask for anything else," she begged.

"All that glitters is not gold, Greta," Mrs. Raczynski chided. "We mustn't be frivolous in these difficult times."

Greta gave up and turned to Addie. Leaning into her friend, she whispered, "Oh! I wish you could come with us today. But you must go spy on Miriam and then tell me everything on Monday at school. I can hardly wait!"

"I will. See you on Monday." Addie hoped that Greta couldn't mind read and tell how much she dreaded seeing Miriam and the boy again. *What if Miriam finds out that I've seen her?* She wanted to pretend that it wasn't real and decided to walk home a different way to avoid running into them. Shutting her eyes, the red line took shape in her mind. She would have to cross Halsted Street, which was very crowded this time of the afternoon. But no mind. Better to face masses of people than risk seeing Miriam and the boy again. She slunk along the streets and kept her eyes to the ground.

Ten

ONCE BACK at the apartment, Addie silently gave the flour to Mama and then prepared to work on her lessons in the back room. Mama gave her a cup of chamomile tea to fend off illness, and watched her leave the kitchen with curious eyes but didn't ask any questions. The back room was always dark by late afternoon, as it had only one small window facing east, but Addie wanted to sit alone in the shadows rather than face anyone in the family. *What if Mama reads Miriam's secret on my face? What if she asks what I saw on the streets? I can't avoid mentioning the boy when I'm used to telling Mama everything I've seen in one great breath.*

Addie couldn't bear the thought of another rough edge in the fabric of her family and resolved to keep Miriam's secret tucked inside her bonnet. Brooding, she drank the tea in the near dark and was about to light a candle to see her sums better when the front door to the apartment creaked slowly open. Next Addie heard whispering and feet shuffling in the front room, then gentle footfalls down the hall. Mama entered the back room and placed her finger to her lips to show Addie to be quiet.

Uncle Ehud entered next, with David, who seemed to be unconscious, draped in his arms. A hard pit formed in Addie's stomach. *David's sick again?* It was only a few days ago that they'd been playing by the lake together. It seemed that the illness had lurked inside David's body this past week, waiting for a moment to strike again. Addie shuddered. The hushed room felt heavy and tight. Addie went over to Moshe's cot, where Uncle Ehud was laying David down, but Mama touched her shoulder and steered her to the door. Reluctantly, she walked to the front room, tears pricking her eyes. *At least now the family won't wonder why I seem upset.* Sammy sat at the table kicking his legs and looking unconcerned, as he took bites out of an apple.

"David went faint at school today, in the middle of a spelling bee, and the teacher had to send an older student out to the shop to fetch Papa!" He sounded excited, as though back from a great adventure. Sammy had become more animated since David had gotten sick, as though some of David's life had seeped into him. "The teacher gave me the shiny red apple sitting on her desk and I got to leave school early with Papa."

Addie sat down next to him. Sammy prattled on about his spelling lesson and the other children at school until she wanted to swat him like a fly. She couldn't focus on any one of the upsetting thoughts on her mind with him buzzing about. *I must be kind to him, though, for he has no mama and now his poor brother's sick again.* Sammy continued eating and talking until only the apple core remained, then nibbled around the seeds and stem, not ready to finish his teacher's special gift. Uncle Ehud and Mama joined them in the front room but didn't sit.

"Go back to the shop now and I'll care for him," Mama was telling Uncle Ehud. "Josef needs you and the boys will be safe with me." She turned to Addie and continued. "You must go find Dr. Goldstein and ask him if there's anything we can do for David. Your uncle already stopped by his house, but Mrs. Goldstein says he's helping an injured worker in a sweatshop at the corner of Taylor and Halsted Streets. It's on the top floor of a building across from a butcher-shop. Do you think you can find it?"

Addie leapt to her feet, almost knocking over a chair.

"Addie!" Mama scolded in her sharp-bright voice. "You must move more slowly and carefully."

Addie silently cursed her long limbs and wished she could be alone in a great open space with no one looking at her. "Yes, Mama." Her face burned with shame. She held perfectly still, punishing her arms and legs for behaving so wildly. Closing her eyes, she tried to imagine the neighborhood around Taylor and Halsted Streets.

Mama seemed sorry now. Her voice became gentle-soft. "Go and find him there. Be quick and careful. Tell him that David's fever's returned and that he fainted at school. He doesn't seem to be coughing as much, but his body is limp from the fever."

"Yes, Mama."

Just then, Miriam opened the door to the apartment. Her face was flushed and bright. But when she saw Uncle Ehud and Sammy her expression darkened. "What is it? Why are you home from the shop, Uncle?" she asked.

Mama answered for him, explaining David's condition. "You must stay and help me care for the boys." Mama's voice sounded crisp and strong, knitting the family together with her direction. Addie was glad that her place was outside in the streets.

Addie looked at Miriam for a long moment before she left. Had the scene in the park been a wild figment of her imagination? But, no, Miriam was wearing the same blue Leghorn straw hat worn by the young woman in the park. Papa had brought the hat home for her last month and said that all the prettiest young women in Chicago were wearing them. The hat's wide brim dipped down in the back and slightly in the front, and had a small black bird sewn onto it. Miriam had only worn it a few times, preferring to admire it on the hat stand. Addie thought it a waste of a pretty thing. If Papa should ever think to give her one she vowed to wear it every day. But Miriam was Papa's favorite and he would probably never give Addie something so lovely. He only gave her gifts at Purim and then usually something small like a lemon candy or hair ribbon.

Miriam caught Addie staring and gave her a quizzical look. Before she could question her, Addie darted out of the apartment, back down the steps and onto the street.

Eleven

A DDIE HURRIED down Adams Street, Papa's words ringing in her ears. "Don't run child! People will wonder if you have parents to teach you manners!" She forced her legs to move slowly and placed each foot firmly on the cobblestones. By the time she reached the corner of Adams and Halsted Streets she was out of breath from the exertion of taking so many tiny, deliberate steps. The chamomile tea sloshed around her belly and she realized that she would need to relieve herself soon.

She turned left at the railway tracks and rested for a moment. *Is this the right direction to go for Taylor Street?* She puzzled at the red line in her head. A milkmaid stood on the street calling out, "Quarts and pints of fresh milk! Milked this morning from my very own cow!" Her voice had a pleasant, musical lilt and Addie tried to guess if she was Irish or Scottish. She still couldn't tell those two accents apart. The maid looked young, about Miriam's age, and Addie wondered if she'd ever been to school. Her dress and bonnet looked tattered and worn, as though she'd traveled to Chicago from the hills of Ireland that very week. A horse pulling a wagon stopped in the middle of the street and several men began yelling at the horseman to move it along. The smell of bread baking somewhere nearby made Addie's stomach growl. And now she also felt a growing heaviness in her bladder and a flicker of panic as she looked around in vain for a privy to use. She tried to concentrate. She pictured David, pale and weak on

Moshe's cot, and then made a quick decision to keep going until she reached the building with the sweatshop. Hustling along, she kept her head bowed low to avoid distractions.

Ten minutes later she reached the corner of Taylor and Halsted Streets and turned around slowly at the edges of the four blocks, trying to figure out where the sweatshop would be. A butcher-shop reeked of blood and animal parts, and directly across the way, facing south, was an ancient-looking building with a small crowd gathered in front.

A stout woman stood talking to a wiry man with a caterpillar mustache near the building's front door, her doughy arms crossed in front of her. Swallowing her shyness, Addie approached them. "I'm looking for Dr. Goldstein. His wife said he's helping an injured worker at a sweatshop near here." The woman remained silent. "Do you know where I might find him?"

The woman wrinkled her nose and looked Addie up and down. She eyed the crisp dress Mama had made for the Jewish holy days last September and Addie's polished boots. Pointing to the door she growled, "You'll find him through there, on the top floor." The woman turned back to the man she'd been talking to.

They put their heads close together and he began to speak quietly. "Doesn't look good. His arm's cut real bad. The doctor's fixed a tourniquet but the damage is done."

Addie's hands felt cold. Her stomach clenched at the thought of ravaged limbs and rivers of blood, and she wondered what a tourniquet was, but she forced herself to enter the building. *David needs the doctor. I must hurry.*

Once she slipped inside she was thrust into pitch dark and felt her bladder tighten in fear. As her eyes adjusted to the dimly lit hall she could make out the stairs. The building was a jumble of noises—whirring machines, people talking and yelling, dogs barking. She made her way to the stairs and climbed, though the steps creaked under her weight and she worried they might collapse beneath her. At the top of the stairs the first door stood ajar and

Addie saw a group of people gathered around in a large attic-like space, with Dr. Goldstein's head bobbing up and down amongst them. The air hung with a stuffy, sour smell of too many people working hard in close quarters. Addie wished she'd brought one of the handkerchiefs Mama stored in dried lavender to cover her mouth and nose. The room was dark and crowded with long tables and chairs, the tables piled with lengths of fabric and scissors and needles and pins. Several dozen women and girls continued at their work despite the accident. They were hunched over and squinting at pieces of cloth held up closely to their faces in the poor light. Addie worried that one woman might stab herself in the eye, she worked so quickly and furiously with the needle darting dangerously close to her face.

Moving slowly, to keep from drawing attention to herself and jostling her aching bladder, Addie walked toward Dr. Goldstein. A young man, a boy really, lay on the floor in the middle of the crowd, looking pale and lifeless. The sight sickened Addie and she took a step back without thinking. Dr. Goldstein was kneeling by the boy, tying a torn-up sheet around his arm. Blood had soaked through the sheet and was dripping onto the floor in two small pools, one on either side of his arm. Addie looked away as her legs threatened to buckle beneath her. *I must give Dr. Goldstein the message and then get out of here!* But another thought filled her with dread. *How can I possibly get all the way home without relieving myself?* A woman and a girl crouched next to the boy's head. The woman spoke to him softly in Yiddish while stroking his hair and the girl whimpered and kept wiping her eyes.

Dr. Goldstein stood up and leaned back with his hands resting on his hips. The boy had closed his eyes. *Is he already dead? Has all the doctor's work gone to waste?* Addie took a step closer and studied the mangled arm. Curiosity overcame her disgust. Dr. Goldstein suddenly noticed her standing a few feet away.

"Addie? What are you doing here? This is no place for a girl like you!" He walked over and placed a hand on her shoulder.

The room hushed for a moment, and the garment workers glanced up at Addie before resuming their work.

"Dr. Goldstein...sir." She coughed and choked the next words out. She suddenly felt fragile and out of her depth, with the garment workers frantically stitching and cutting all around her and the boy whose life was held together by threads. "Mrs. Goldstein told Uncle Ehud I'd find you here." She paused again. "It's David. He's made a turn for the worse and Mama's afraid that the illness has come back. He's feverish and he fainted at school."

Dr. Goldstein looked grave. He ran his hands over his eyes and let them rest there for a moment. "Tell your uncle I'll come see David in the evening, after this poor boy's stable." He sighed, his voice tired-soft. "There's no telling how long that'll take, but I'll stop by your apartment on my way home." He smiled weakly and Addie smiled back, grateful for his kindness. "Are you all right, child?"

Addie felt her bladder tighten again, like a balloon that would surely burst soon. Could she say something? Instead, she nodded quickly and asked, "Is the boy...will he survive? And what's happened to his arm?"

"He nearly cut off his arm with one of the heavy knives used to shape the cloth. Poor boy had already worked sixteen hours straight to help his father meet the contractor's demands, and under this terrible light his hand slipped. I've stopped the bleeding for now, so he should live. Only he won't be fit for much work again."

Addie thought of the one-legged beggar who stood on the street corner two blocks south of their apartment. *Will this boy be forced to beg for his dinner as well? Or will his family be able to scratch out enough to feed him?* She looked closely at the nearly severed arm, trying to understand how the cloth could keep the boy from bleeding out. She swayed from side to side, focusing on the boy to distract herself from the growing pressure in her bladder.

"The sight doesn't frighten you, child?" Dr. Goldstein asked.

Addie shook her head. "Come here, then." He bent down and pointed to the boy's forearm. "This cloth is what's called a tourniquet—it's a three-sided piece of linen that can be folded many different ways and then tied tightly around a bleeding limb, to keep the blood from flowing out. Do you see?" Addie knelt down and studied the piece of linen, amazed that a simple piece of fabric could save the boy's life. "If seeing wounds doesn't bother you, perhaps you have a future as a nurse," Dr. Goldstein remarked. "Or maybe even a doctor—there are women now excelling in medicine. But don't tell your father I said that." Addie nodded as she stood up, then bounced up and down on her toes. "Addie? What is it child?" He smiled at her. "Do you need a privy?" Relief flooded though her, as she nodded vigorously and felt her face flush with embarrassment.

Dr. Goldstein addressed the girl who was sitting by the injured boy's head. "Addie needs the privy. Will you take her?" The girl nodded, and Addie prayed she would get up quickly. Addie followed her through the knot of garment workers, out into the hall and down the stairs.

"Is that your brother? The one who's hurt?" Addie asked gingerly, not wanting to upset the girl, but curious.

"Yes," she answered quietly. "Max." She inhaled sharply and hiccoughed. "He'd been working too long. Mama told him to go to bed, but Papa says the big garment factories downtown are about to stop buying from the small shops, so we need to get as much work done now as we possibly can." Her voice tightened and became a high whisper. "Mama says we already owe the butcher so much that he's threatened to stop giving us meat...and we've already taken in three extra boarders. But Mama says the months come too quickly now to pay for the rent." Her voice trailed off.

They walked through the back door of the building to the outside. Addie's family had their very own water closet, right inside their apartment. Mama scrubbed it every other day to keep it clean and from smelling badly. Addie had used outdoor privies before, but always felt exposed and dirty when she did. The girl handed her a thick wooden stick. "Sometimes you need this to fend off stray dogs when you come out," she said shyly, almost apologizing. Addie raced to the small wooden shack, pulled down her stockings, hitched up her dress so that it wouldn't touch the dirt floor or splintered wooden walls, and finally emptied her full bladder. The relief made her feel giddy and relaxed.

Back outside again, with no stray dogs in sight, Addie realized how slight and pinched the girl looked, as though her arms and face had been taken in by sewing pins and extra stitches. They walked to the building in silence and Addie wondered if the girl was ashamed at all by what she'd said. She wanted to fill the emptiness between them and comfort the girl.

"Dr. Goldstein's a good doctor. The best. He'll take good care of your brother and make him right again. He's been taking care of my cousin who came home again from school today with a terrible fever and cough."

"School?" The girl stopped and looked at Addie. Then, as if embarrassed by her reaction, she continued walking.

Addie's stomach tightened. She knew that lots of children worked for their families instead of going to school but she'd never imagined this—working so many hours that you almost cut off your own arm and then still not having enough money to pay the butcher!

They climbed the stairs in silence. Addie wanted to take the girl's hand and give her a comforting squeeze, but she couldn't tell if the girl liked her or not. Back inside the sweatshop the girl rushed back to her brother's side before Addie could thank her.

Dr. Goldstein called over to Addie. "Run along, now. Tell Ehud I'll come later. This is no place for you, Addie." He smiled. "Or shall I call you *Ärztin*, the lady doctor?"

Addie blushed and looked down, then turned to leave. *But why are other children working here if it's no place for me? That poor boy laying on the floor...and why don't these girls have primers and study the seven continents and the rules of English grammar?* Addie's mind teemed with a torrent of new questions.

She ran down the stairs and out the front door, forgetting Papa's words about being ladylike. Once outside, she squinted against the bright sun and kept running north along Halsted Street toward her own apartment as fast as she could. The outdoor privy had made her skin feel itchy and rough. But she could also feel a spot of brightness inside her, a new sense of hope and vibrancy. *Why do I have this feeling?* she asked herself…and then she knew. Dr. Goldstein had planted a seed in her mind. *Could I really be nurse…or a doctor, myself?*

Twelve

A S PROMISED, Dr. Goldstein arrived that night with more medicine for David. He told Uncle Ehud that the boy at the sweatshop had died after all, from losing so much blood. After listening to David's chest with a stethoscope, he shook his head and told the family that David was suffering from consumption and would need uninterrupted rest to recover. David continued to run a fever all through the night and Mama couldn't even get him to sip a little broth. Uncle Ehud and Sammy slept in the front room, with David on Moshe's cot in the back bedroom, and Moshe curled up on the floor in the hall.

In the morning Addie lingered in the washroom and listened to the noises of the apartment. She felt sad about the boy at the sweatshop but wasn't sure how to talk with her family about him. In the front room Papa and Uncle Ehud discussed the next shipment of derbies from New York, while Mama fussed over David in the back bedroom. A newspaper rustled as Moshe read the latest reports on the strikes.

Addie walked out to the front room and sat down next to Moshe at the table, wanting to be near her brother, then picked up her quilt and pretended to study the stitches. She had managed to sew eight pieces together, though some of the stitching looked crooked. As long as her hands were busy and she kept quiet, Papa wouldn't notice her. She made three whip stitches on the edging. They looked loose and messy, like big, sloppy Ss. She paused and stole a glance at Moshe's paper. A large advertisement for Sears, Roebuck & Co. took up half the back page. Mama had discussed this new company with their neighbor Mrs. Hardy just the week before. The store had been founded here in Chicago earlier in the year and was supposed to make the lives of Americans easier, with more comfort and leisure. Mama was skeptical about the company, but Mrs. Hardy said it would help turn Chicago into the greatest city in the world. Addie looked back at her quilt and listened to Papa and Uncle Ehud, hoping that their conversation would turn from the family business to the strikes.

"Tomorrow I'll inventory the back stock and we'll put another order in with Mr. Lockheed," Uncle Ehud said.

Papa seemed irritated about something, as though a mosquito was flying around his ears. "But Ehud, how can we know if people will still buy our hats with all this trouble in the city? The union attacking workers for doing their jobs now...attacking the very people who want to work and make the city run? Do they realize we've only just come out of a depression and this is no time to disrupt the new industries?" Spit flew from his mouth as he spoke. Addie pitied any mosquito that tried to buzz near Papa. "Perhaps people will begin to move further west, where there's less danger and one's allowed to work in peace." His voice trailed off and he looked out the window with eagle eyes, searching for signs of the trouble he spoke about.

Addie's body stiffened at the mention of the strikes. She kept her eyes trained on a new quilt piece and hoped that Papa and Uncle Ehud would keep up the conversation.

"Ha! Less danger in the west!" Uncle Ehud laughed, but it was a bitter kind of laughter. "Josef, think of the train robberies and towns with no sheriff. Those who are afraid will stay in the city. And there's no work in the west now...the gold rush is long over. The police here have a handle on the workingmen. They showed that last night." Uncle Ehud sat forward in his chair and placed his elbows on his knees.

Papa continued, as though he'd barely heard his brother. "The city is growing wilder all the time. And now the workers are striking day in and day out—as though they lived high on the hog in their own countries. They should be grateful for the work and stay home at night."

Uncle Ehud grunted. Addie couldn't tell if the grunt meant that he agreed with Papa or just wanted to end the conversation.

"But, Papa," Moshe ventured. "The people in Packingtown have no way of knowing how long their work will last. They have families to feed and rent to pay." Addie's hands tingled uncomfortably at Moshe's words. She feared for her brother, testing Papa's angry mood with his opinions. Moshe swallowed hard, but continued. "And, truly, how can you blame the workers from the factory, who might be able to make more for their families?" He paused again, then said carefully, "The police shouldn't have fired on them last night."

Addie's heart quickened. *Police fired on the workers last night?*

Papa stood up and began to pace around the silent room. "Addie!" he shouted. Addie's face burned at the sound of her name.

"Yes, Papa?" Her voice shook.

"Where is Miriam?"

Addie looked around and suddenly realized that Miriam had been gone since just before dawn. *Oh no!*

"I don't know, Papa. Perhaps she went into school early to help her teacher with the assignments." Addie's mind began to work quickly, going over the details of Miriam's days and wondering how to keep Papa's anger from burning up the apartment. Miriam had been leaving early and arriving home well after school ended, with no explanation of her whereabouts.

"Papa, she's fine," Moshe reassured him. "Addie's right… Miriam's been helping the teacher before school and after class is let out."

Does Moshe know the truth and is he covering up for Miriam, too?

Uncle Ehud interrupted. "Josef, if we can return for a moment

62

to the shop." He sounded impatient. "Are you suggesting that I put Lockheed off?"

"No, Ehud, no. We can't put off another order or we won't have inventory left."

Uncle Ehud huffed. "Well, yes. That was my point."

Papa began to pace again. Addie held the quilt against her lap and continued to make loose stitches along the new piece. Part of her enjoyed Papa and Uncle Ehud's arguments. They reminded her of little boys playing tug-of-war in the schoolyard. *Back and forth, back and forth.* As long as they were both occupied with each other, and the rope between them, they wouldn't notice her, or Moshe, or Miriam's absence.

"But sales have been down and we don't know how long certain styles will remain popular with men in America," Papa continued. "So I don't know."

"Oh, Josef! You drive me mad. If this is left up to you, poor Lockheed will waste away waiting for an answer from us."

Moshe turned the pages of the newspaper and coughed.

"What is it, Moshe? Do you have something to say?" Papa's voice was rough like sandpaper.

"No, Papa."

"What then?"

"Nothing, Papa. Perhaps I'm getting a cold."

Addie knew the tone in Papa's voice. He wanted to fight with Moshe, but Moshe knew better than to fight with Papa when he was so irritated.

"You think these working men and anarchists have a valid point, do you?" Papa needled Moshe.

"Well, Papa." Moshe spoke very slowly and kept his voice level. "The Constitution protects the rights of American citizens to assemble and speak their minds freely. So, whether or not I agree with the anarchists, they're allowed to gather and protest their working conditions. It was wrong for the police to open fire on them, just to make an example."

Papa grew red in the face but stayed silent. He turned toward the window and Moshe went back to reading the paper. Addie held her breath, secretly hoping that Moshe had beaten Papa in the argument. She remembered the people at the sweatshop. *Shouldn't workers be able to make a living for their families? And shouldn't children be able to go to school, instead of having to work in factories, just so their families can eat?*

After a while, Papa spoke again, his voice quiet-hard. "If they only worked more and kept away from drinking, they'd make enough money and stop their complaining. Most of them were used to much harder work in the old country." He turned back to Moshe. "It was there that we worked like savages. You can't possibly remember because you're too young."

Moshe pushed back his chair and stood up. "I'm sorry, Papa. I'm only telling you what's written in the American Constitution." He sounded bitter and angry and—without saying goodbye to Mama or anyone else—he picked up his cap and left the apartment. The door slammed shut.

Papa and Uncle Ehud looked at each other and Papa shrugged. Mama came out of the back room and looked at Papa intently. "What did you say, Josef? Why did he leave like that...with the door slamming?"

Papa ignored her question. "What I'd like to know is where Miriam is. Did she ask you to go to school early?"

"Yes, Josef. She's been helping her teacher in the hopes of getting a letter for a teaching position." She paused. "But what about Moshe?"

Papa sighed. "We were discussing politics and we disagreed. There was an incident at the McCormick factory yesterday. Some of the strikers confronted the workers who'd taken their jobs and the police shot two of them."

Mama sucked in her breath. "No!" she exclaimed. She looked down at Addie, as though just seeing her for the first time. "Go to school now, Addie. Let me get your lunch pail. Go now or you'll be late."

Thirteen

THAT EVENING, Miriam arrived home late again, this time breathless and worried. Moshe was out selling afternoon papers, which had been more popular than ever with all the workers' protests. Papa didn't have a chance to question Miriam as she burst into the front room.

"Mama, Papa...these notices are all over the streets." She handed a sheet of paper to Papa. "The socialists have organized a rally tonight at Haymarket Square to protest the killings yesterday," she said, gasping for breath.

Papa examined the sheet, crumpled it in one hand, then threw it on the floor. "When will they stop, Sara? How much longer must we endure these disruptions?" Papa scowled at Mama, as though she had personally printed and handed out all the notices.

Mama said she was feeling unwell and must rest. Her eyes looked small and wet. "You'll have to eat bread tonight," she said to Addie and Papa and Miriam in her soft-cold voice, then shuffled down the dark hall. Papa put on his derby and left the apartment.

Miriam watched from the window as he walked down the street and then turned to Addie. "I should follow him and see if he's all right."

Addie shrugged, though she felt a strange knot form in the center of her belly. *Why is Miriam going out again? Doesn't she usually prefer to be home?* Addie remembered the boy in the park but kept her mouth shut.

As soon as Miriam left the apartment, Addie felt cold and lonely. She longed to creep into Mama's bed and ask her to sing soft lullabies in German, or tell stories of when Addie was a baby. Then she remembered Uncle Chaim. *He'll be at the Haymarket Square with the other protesters!* She picked up the crumpled paper on the floor and read,

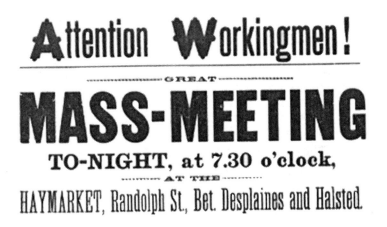

Attention Workingmen!

GREAT

MASS-MEETING

TO-NIGHT, at 7.30 o'clock,

AT THE

HAYMARKET, Randolph St., Bet. Desplaines and Halsted.

Addie knew she'd find him there. Without another thought, she raced to the hat hook, pulled down Papa's long winter coat and navy bowler hat, dressed herself in the little geschäftsmann disguise, and hurried out of the apartment and down the stairs before she could change her mind.

Addie knew where to find Haymarket Square, and ran down Desplaines Street looking for the best place to turn west. The red line didn't appear that evening—perhaps because she was afraid and her heart seemed to be beating up in her head. She shivered as a light rain fell and pulled Papa's bowler hat down and around her ears. She was careful to keep her braids tucked up under the hat.

At the end of the block people were gathered in a tightly knit crowd. In the distance, the street was lit up so brightly that it looked like daytime. *That must be the workers' rally! Uncle Chaim is there. Maybe those men who were killed yesterday were his friends.* Addie kept moving toward Haymarket Square, like a moth fluttering ever closer to a burning flame. *I must find Uncle Chaim.*

At least two dozen torches blazed in the block between Halsted and Desplaines Streets. Addie looked for a dark place to hide, but the place was lit up like a great sun. She shook with fear as she scanned the crowd for Uncle Chaim.

A man stood on top of a wooden crate in the back of a parked wagon and spoke to the crowd in a fierce-bright voice. She caught the loudest words of his speech, "...defend yourselves, your lives, your futures." The people cheered for him and whistled. Cold rain pelted Addie's cheeks. Some members of the crowd began to leave. *Where is Uncle Chaim?*

Addie ducked into the thickest part of the crowd where she could conceal herself. She hunched her shoulders down and leaned forward to look smaller. Trousers and coats and caps of grown men were everywhere, but she saw no faces, nothing familiar to calm her racing pulse. Then she lost her footing and tripped on someone's ankle. She began toppling toward the ground but grabbed another man's heavy, dark coat to pull herself up. She clung to the coat for support and the man never seemed to notice her. The rough wool felt comforting in her hand—something she could hold onto in the slithering crowd. Addie felt very hot, as though coming down with a fever. Her cheeks flushed. The shouts of several men pummeled her ears. She was desperate to find an open street and cool air.

Somehow she had to get back to the sidewalk, where she could see the faces of the men in the crowd and find Uncle Chaim. But pulling herself away seemed impossible and her feet moved beneath her on the same current that carried all the men. She had been swallowed up by a writing animal. *What would Mama say if she knew I was here? Papa?* The thought made her eyes sting.

All at once, a line of policemen appeared in the shadows of the square. The silver stars and buttons on their coats glimmered in the light of the Lyceum Theater. One of them stepped forward and announced, "In the name of the law, I command you to disperse." A red glare arced above the crowd and Addie heard an explosion. The buildings along Randolph Street shook, while men screamed and horses whinnied in terror, and a few moments later gunshots split the night air. More gunshots, and then the sounds of chaos. Addie couldn't tell where the noise had come from and covered her ears with the palms of her hands and burrowed her chin into her chest. The shots shook inside her body. For a moment she wondered if she'd been hit. The chanting gave way to shouts and gasps. The crowd jerked and shuddered. Addie managed to squeeze through several knots of men and finally made her way to the outer edge of the crowd. Another loud explosion down the street shook the night and she ducked into the closest alley.

Away from the crowd, she felt the cold down in her bones. The prickly heat from the crowd turned icy on the night breeze. She leaned against a brick wall in the alley and tried to catch her breath. *I must get home as soon as I can.* She forgot about Uncle Chaim then and could only think of Mama. The shouting continued and Addie heard piercing screams from a man. Her heart galloped. She closed her eyes and willed the red line to appear and tell her where to go. Light blazed from dozens of moving torches and she felt disoriented, not sure which side of the street was east from west.

The crowd began to disperse. A few men ran down the alley, panting as they felt their way through the dark night. "Run!" one of the men shout-whispered. Addie wanted to join them, to put distance between herself and this dreadful place. But her legs buckled beneath her.

Men emptied the square now, moving in all directions at once, some crawling along the ground on their hands and knees. She could see several bodies lying on the street and her stomach twisted in on itself. Her chest heaved and she vomited, the hot fluid burning her throat and mouth. *Are those men hurt or dead?* She thought of Dr. Goldstein. *Should I find him and bring him back here to take care of them?* Uncle Chaim could be one of them. Not sure what to do, Addie turned away from the street but was afraid of the dark alley. Her eyes began to adjust to the deep night. *How did those men run so easily through the alley just moments before?* She moved slowly and deliberately, making as little sound as possible and stuck close to the building walls for support. Bile burned the roof of her mouth. She wished so much that she had stayed at home with Mama and David in their safe apartment.

More men passed her by and Addie felt relieved that they didn't seem to notice her. The red line flashed in her mind strongly now. She knew how to get home. Moving faster, she felt her courage return. Up ahead at the next cross street more torches lit up the darkness. Men yelled at one another and darted around, like bats out hunting for their midnight dinner.

Addie ran several more blocks, avoiding the streetlights and crowds as much as possible and slipping through the shadows. She picked up speed and her feet became light on the cobblestoned street. Just as she turned onto Adams, Moshe appeared, looking frantic with worry.

"Addie, come quickly." He grabbed her by the shoulders with both hands, as though afraid of losing her. "Mama's worried sick and Papa's still out. We have to hurry home before he discovers that you're missing."

Addie's chest burned as she ran, this time ahead of Moshe and not caring if she left him behind. The image of Papa raging in a fury burned in her mind's eye. All at once, a gust of wind stole Papa's bowler from her head. The hat cartwheeled down the street but Moshe called, "Never mind! There're more where that came from!" His voice sounded harsh-cold and Addie's throat ached with sadness and regret.

The streets were quieter near the apartment. Without any hesitation, Addie raced up the steps and through the front door. The apartment seemed especially bright, with all the lamps lit like a vigil. For a moment, Addie flashed back to the torches at the Haymarket. She thrust Papa's coat onto the hook and heard Moshe struggling up the last flight of stairs. Mama and Miriam stood in the front room, watching her silently with drawn faces. She walked as silently and quickly as she could to the back bedroom, lay on the bed, covered herself with the gray blanket, and tried to breathe quietly.

She could hear the murmur of conversation from down the hall, muted but intense. Suddenly the door slammed shut and Papa's boots were stomping around. Then the deep thunder of his voice came. "And where in heaven's name is my navy bowler?"

Fourteen

D AVID SAVED the family from Papa's wrath that night. Mama made shushing sounds and said, "Josef, you must keep quiet for the boy."

Finally, Papa's rage burned out and the apartment became a fireplace with only cold ashes left in the grate. Addie lay under the blanket, quaking with fear, until morning—when Mama found her burning with fever. She looked at Addie with cold, worried eyes but never said anything.

For two days Addie stayed in bed. Her body ached from the fever and from keeping still. Mama wouldn't let her go to temple on Sunday or to school on Monday. She checked Addie's fever and looked down her throat and brought her broth, but wouldn't speak to her. David lay across from her on Moshe's cot, coughing pitifully and sputtering on the broth Mama brought. Addie could hear Papa and Mama and Uncle Ehud whispering just out of earshot. *They must be worried about David or perhaps they're discussing what happened at the Haymarket.* Papa's missing bowler hat seemed to have been forgotten.

On the afternoon of the second day, when the whole family except Mama and David were gone, Addie crept to the front room to sit on the sofa and work on her quilt. The sound of Mama chopping onions and potatoes in the kitchen lulled her to sleep. When she woke up, a blanket had been tucked around her.

Moshe was in the kitchen, saying in his quiet-urgent voice, "It's here in the paper, Mama. One of the anarchists threw a bomb into the crowd of policemen at the Haymarket!"

"*Mein Gott!*" Mama cried. "What else does it say?"

"The bomb killed a policeman, and then the police opened fire on the crowd of protesters and shot four of them. Dozens of other policemen and protesters were injured. Some of them may well die."

Mama sighed heavily. Addie closed her eyes and pretended to be asleep, in case they came through to the front room. But she kept her ears pricked for more news.

"Were there more protests these past two nights? You don't think..." Mama stopped herself. *What had she been about to say?*

Moshe responded quickly. "I think that, if Uncle Chaim were hurt or killed, one of his friends would've come to tell us. He might be in danger, but I think he must be alive." Moshe sounded so grown up and kind, and Addie's chest swelled with love for him. How she longed for Mama and Moshe to forgive her for running off the other night and to take her back into their hearts! "And no," Moshe continued, "there haven't been any more protests since the night before last at the Haymarket."

"Please continue reading," Mama pleaded, her voice shrill with anticipation and worry.

Moshe cleared his throat and read from the paper. "The police are looking into the bombing and rounding up suspects who have been involved with union activities. They have issued a curfew for the nighttime so people are no longer allowed to travel after dark. Seven men have already been arrested and are being held in the Cook County jail until further notice."

Addie heard Mama sit down heavily on the kitchen stool. *What does this all mean? Bombs? Opening fire on a crowd? Arrests?* A shiver ran down Addie's spine. *I heard that very bomb explode and those shots fired. I was there, in the Haymarket!*

"Your father will be so angry. Why did the protesters have to throw a bomb at the policemen?" Mama sounded hurt-worn.

"The workers have been pushed too hard," Moshe said. "It isn't right, Mama. They shouldn't be the beasts of the rich."

"But the violence...I thought we left that behind in the old country. And now Chaim is involved."

"We should not speak too much about him, Mama. We can only pray that he's not rounded up and tried. It seems to me they'll be looking to arrest anyone involved." Moshe sounded angry. "It isn't right. Any of it. Workers should be given a fair wage." Moshe's voice stopped abruptly. Then he continued, his voice lower. "But perhaps you're right, Mama. I'm not so sure violence will accomplish much in the end. The unions need to strengthen themselves, with the law and more politicians supporting them. And yet..." his voice trailed off, as though he were in deep thought.

"What is it, Moshe?" Mama asked.

"Oh, Mama, this country is like a puzzle with all the right pieces but they can't be arranged correctly." Addie thought of her quilt, the squares that didn't quite fit. "The laws allow people to vote and speak freely but then the companies have more power because they can give and take jobs. People must be able to work to feed their families. If you're hungry, what use is it to speak freely?"

Addie sat up straighter and opened her eyes. *What would Papa say to this? Surely he doesn't agree with Moshe and Mama.* He believed that immigrants who complained about their lot in America should go back to Europe on the next boat.

"We're lucky to own our own shop," Mama said. "But I watch from the window...I see the people in the street, with no shoes on their feet in the cold, the children mere shadows from lack of food and warmth. The mothers with the look of terrible desperation in their eyes. There is nothing worse than watching your children go hungry. I saw it in Germany and hoped to be rid of that sight forever." She sighed. "I must check on the children, Moshe."

Mama walked out into the front room and saw that Addie was awake. She came over and kissed her forehead and smoothed her hair.

"I'm sorry, Mama," Addie whispered.

Mama's eyes looked stern but the edges of her mouth tipped upward. Addie grabbed Mama's hand from her head and kissed it.

"Tomorrow you may return to school, Addie. I think you've rested enough and it's important to keep up with your studies."

Moshe came into the front room with the newspaper under his arm. "Better today, Addie?"

She nodded and smiled shyly at him, but his expression was distant and blank and revealed nothing of what he was thinking.

Fifteen

ADDIE WANTED to hear more conversations about the Haymarket, but not with Papa raging around the tight apartment, shouting to no one in particular, "People dead for no good reason! Now we may be forced to close down the shop!"

Addie sat on her bed braiding her hair. In the front room Moshe was reading a book about American law and poking Papa with difficult questions. "But, Papa, you've read the Constitution and its amendments, haven't you? American citizens are free to gather and speak their minds."

Papa paced around the small room with growing agitation. "Moshe, do not involve yourself in such political matters. The shop is more important to our family than what the unions do. Just leave it!"

Addie stared at the brush in her hand and felt the skin on the back of her neck bristle. A part of her wanted Moshe to say something more to Papa, but then she also dreaded the storm of Papa's darkening mood.

"And the paper says that less than 2,500 people attended the rally, not the 20,000 expected, so why would the police be so aggressive...when the crowd was so much smaller than planned for?" Moshe poked again.

With her hair now braided in two tight plaits that wound about her ears, Addie crept into the front room, hoping they would take no notice of her.

"How the police behave is no concern of ours!" Papa shouted, and Moshe, who seemed to be tiring of the conversation, responded, "Yes, Papa. Of course." He turned the newspaper over.

Mama stood outside the kitchen door, looking back and forth at each of them as she wiped her hands on her apron. "You tell the boy to be an American, and now he shows interest in American law. Let him be, Josef. He is almost a grown man." Her voice was hard-cold, a tone Addie rarely heard Mama use with Papa.

Papa stared at Mama, then put on his derby and walked out the apartment door.

At school, Addie read her primer with renewed interest. *What does it mean to live in this country where people are supposed to be free and yet are killed for speaking their minds? And why are the anarchists calling for violence? And where, oh where, is Uncle Chaim?* The thought of Uncle Chaim made her stomach and throat tighten with worry. Miss Green dismissed the students for afternoon recess and Greta urged her to come outside to play hopscotch.

"Come on, silly! Close your book and let's play."

"I'll come in a minute. Go on without me," Addie urged. She needed to think without being interrupted. Just last month Addie would have been the first one out of the classroom when Miss Green called for recess. *How much I've changed in just these past few weeks.* Addie thought of her younger self with a sharp pang of longing.

She sat with her primer opened to an empty page and worked on two math problems. *$2,500 \div 8 = 312.5$. So there is about a one in three hundred chance that Uncle was killed at the Haymarket.* Addie used her pen to mark dots on her page—one, two, three, four, five, six... She wanted to see what three hundred and twelve dots looked like, but her hand started to cramp at forty so she stopped. *And $20,000 \div 2,500 = 8$, so the crowd was only one eighth* *the size of what the police expected.* Numbers swirled about in Addie's head. *Eight...eight...eight hours...one-eighth the size...eight...What does it all mean?* She wanted to cry with frustration, but instead she slammed her primer shut and ran outside to find Greta for the last five minutes of recess.

Addie took the long way to the hat shop after school, through the park and along the market. She counted her steps. Every eight steps she would stop and look around for a clue or a sign or something unusual. *Maybe if I tell Mama more stories about what I see on the streets she'll love me completely again. Maybe the number eight will help me.* Walking slowly along Peoria Street, she wanted to take in as much of the city as she could, before arriving at the gloomy shop. Eight steps—a carriage driver whipped his skinny horse for not moving fast enough through the traffic. Another eight steps—an older woman, bent from farm work in the old country, approached Addie. "Child, where will I find an apothecary?"

Her words seemed to take great effort. The woman began to cough violently and she pulled out a filthy gray cloth to block her mouth. She held up her hand to Addie, asking her to wait while she finished coughing. Addie wanted to squirm away from her but stood still.

Mama had explained to Addie what the word apothecary meant, so she told the woman where the drugstore was, a block down on Jackson Street. The streets felt hushed and tight since the riot the week before. Men and women looked down and moved quickly through the city. Another eight steps—Addie paused in front of the new church under construction. A harsh sound startled her.

"Pssstttttt."

Addie jumped back and caught herself on an iron railing used to tie up horses.

"Addie? Addie? Is it really you?"

Addie's heart began to race and she clutched her lunch pail with both hands. The voice sounded so familiar, and yet how could it be? *Maybe eight is a magical number.* Under the wooden scaffolding, in the back entrance of the church, stood Uncle Chaim. He looked taller than Addie remembered but also bent over a bit, like a tree growing on a windy hill.

He retreated back under cover. Addie's arms and head flooded with a crackling warmth. She ran towards him, then thought better of it and slowed down. After glancing around to make sure no one was watching, she slid beneath the scaffolding.

"Oh, Uncle!" Addie whispered and restrained herself from hugging him. She studied him carefully. His beard looked bushy and wild and his left cheek was smudged with black grease.

He beamed at Addie. "Bärchen! You're a welcome sight to see! Oh, how I've missed you all."

The sounds on the street seemed too loud and Addie wished she could be alone in a quiet place with her uncle. She wanted to ask him all about the Haymarket—where he'd been standing and what he'd seen and if he knew the man who'd thrown the bomb into the police and if he knew the men who'd been killed. She wanted to tell him all that she'd seen during that terrifying night. But she held the swarm of thoughts and questions inside, afraid that if she mentioned the riot he would disappear and she'd never be able to find him again. She longed to somehow attach herself to him, or perhaps climb into his coat pocket, so that she would never lose him again.

"How are your Mama and Papa? Moshe and Miriam?"

Addie nodded, suddenly realizing that he must be worried about Mama and the others. But how could he ask about Papa in the same breath as Mama—the man who'd kept him away from the family? *Is he hiding his hatred of Papa from me? Or perhaps he understands Papa better than I do.*

78

"We're well, though David's been ill. And Papa's been angry these days..." Addie paused and searched her uncle's face. *Can I speak openly with him about the riot?* She decided to play it safe. "David's coughing comes in fits that he can't stop on his own. And quite often there's blood when he coughs. He can only rest on Moshe's cot and drink Mama's broth."

Uncle Chaim nodded and touched her hand. "David's strong like you, Addie." He stood up.

Is he leaving already? Addie's mind reeled. *I must find out where he's staying and how I can see him again.*

Uncle Chaim looked so tired, yet his eyes were still kind and playful. "I've been staying with friends from the railway, but I'd like to see your mama, if you think it might be possible."

Addie shook her head. "I don't think Papa'll allow it. He's angry...about the strikes and the violence." She looked down, afraid to see Uncle Chaim's reaction.

He stood up and paced beneath the scaffolding. He spoke more quickly now. "Addie, if I send a note along with you—so that you wouldn't have to speak a message to your mama, but she might know that I'm safe and well—would that be too much to ask?"

Addie swallowed, her mind racing as she thought of Papa's lost bowler hat and Mama's silence in the days after the Haymarket and the growing rift she felt with Mama. "No, of course not, Uncle. Papa'll surely stay late at the hat shop and Mama's been worried about you."

"Very well. Do you have a slip of paper in your school bag and a pencil I might borrow?"

Addie pulled open her satchel and tore a sheet of paper from the back of her primer. Uncle used the primer as a hard surface to write on and scrawled out a few sentences. He wrote very quickly, folded the paper and handed it to Addie. She placed it carefully in her pocket.

"I meet some of my friends here behind this church in the afternoons. I might be here another time if you're on your way from school." He winked at Addie. "You should go now, before the family wonders where you are."

Addie hugged him. "I miss you. I hope you can come back soon," she said quietly, trying to keep her voice steady.

Uncle Chaim winked again and swallowed. "Go on." His voice was kind-warm.

She took one last look at her uncle, bit her lip to stop herself from crying and shuffled back out onto the street.

Sixteen

ADDIE SKIPPED along the wooden sidewalk across Adams to Halsted Street. Happiness bubbled up at the thought of Uncle Chaim and the note lodged way down in the depths of her pocket. High, tiny clouds covered the sun and the streets seemed almost empty, so she could race as fast as her legs wanted to go. *Uncle Chaim is alive and I have his note to Mama, which means he might make things right with Papa and come home soon!* She ran all the way to the hat shop and arrived out of breath, told Papa she must go home to study for the class spelling bee, and then galloped all the way home.

As she approached the apartment Widow Adler called out from her perch on the front stairs. "Out on the streets alone again? The city is not safe for children. Surely your parents aren't letting you out alone?"

Addie made herself talk to the widow, though her clothes smelled musty, like an old shoe. "I'm on my way home from the shop and won't be going out again." Addie spoke quickly and quietly, hoping the widow wouldn't question her further.

"Hmmmph," the woman grunted.

Mama was sitting on the sofa hemming what looked like heavy curtains. *What will Mama think of the note? Will she be angry at me for agreeing to bring it home? Surely not.*

"What are you working on?" Addie asked, trying to keep her voice calm. Realizing that she might not have much time to give Mama the note, she asked, "Where's David?" without letting Mama answer her first question.

"He's resting in the back room. Miriam's with him."

The apartment was quiet, so Addie decided to act. "Mama, here. This is for you." She reached down to the bottom of her pocket and felt Uncle Chaim's note. Mama looked up from her sewing. Before she could reconsider, Addie thrust the note into her hand and whispered, "I saw Uncle Chaim today and he asked me to give this to you."

Mama's face brightened, and then she caught herself and her face became drawn in and hard to read. She looked around, making sure no one was in earshot, then leaned in close to Addie.

"Where did you see him? Is he all right?" Her words rushed out, like steam being released from a vent.

"Behind the church on Adams Street," Addie whispered. "He seems all right, Mama." Mama laid aside the curtains and took the note into the kitchen to read. Addie desperately wanted to follow her, but then Miriam called out.

"Addie, is that you? Are you home? Come here!"

Addie pushed open the door to the back bedroom. Miriam sat on the edge of Moshe's cot where David lay. "Addie, will you stay and watch David while I go out to the store?"

The boy in the park flashed in Addie's mind as she felt a surge of anger. *Miriam's going to meet the boy again. I know it! How can she think about him when David's so sick and Uncle Chaim's out on the streets?* She wanted to stall Miriam, to keep her safe at home with the family. *We can't have another person in this family disappear or fall ill or run away!*

"I don't know, Miriam. I should ask Mama if she needs help first." Mama wouldn't start cooking the evening meal for at least another hour, but Addie didn't want to let Miriam leave so easily. The bedroom felt warm and close, and Addie's face flushed in the stifling air.

"Addie, please." Miriam stood up quickly and took her hand and squeezed it. She looked at Addie with pleading eyes. David's labored breathing filled the quiet room. Miriam's brown eyes glistened with tears.

"Miriam, what's wrong? Are you worried about David?" Addie demanded.

David coughed once in his sleep and rolled over.

Miriam spoke quickly and with a hushed-bright voice. "Oh Addie! What should I do?" She wrung her hands together. "I...I...I may be going away soon, but you mustn't tell anyone or Papa will get angry." She looked frightened, as if she'd already said too much. "You won't tell, will you? I might not go. I feel terrible leaving, with David so ill and Papa so upset and so much trouble with the workers, but..."

Addie's heart beat against her chest like a wild stallion trying to escape his harness. *Miriam leave us? How could she leave us...and leave Papa?* If Miriam ran off, Papa would never let her come home again. A cold nub began to form in the center of Addie's belly. She imagined Miriam's place at the dinner table empty and let out a long wail. Miriam covered Addie's mouth with her hand.

"Shhhhhh!" She sounded angry. "Be quiet or Mama'll come."

Addie pulled up the hem of her dress and dried her tears, though they kept flowing uncontrollably. Her body shuddered as she held the wailing inside. She didn't dare speak, only held onto Miriam's waist. Miriam spoke quickly, her words coming out in a torrent, like blood from a deep puncture.

"I have to get away from here...from Papa and this tiny apartment and from the city with all its mess and craziness. I met a young man who has a claim in Dakota Territory, and we could go there soon and start a family and I wouldn't have to teach school, after all. But of course that means leaving all of you...and Papa wouldn't let me back, ever. I know that for sure. So it'll be like dying from this life and being born again, only this time with wide open space and...and Clarence."

There, she said it, Addie thought. *His name is Clarence. C-L-A-R-E-N-C-E. Eight letters! Eight again…* The letters like a horrible spell that had been cast and could never be undone. *Now I know for sure that he's real, a real person who wants to marry my sister.* Addie kept crying silently as Miriam described the land in Dakota Territory and her imagined new life.

"His brothers have already moved there and expect him… us to join them—the way Uncle Ehud moved to Chicago first and then Papa came."

Addie didn't know what to say. Miriam sounded happy when she talked about her new life, but Addie could only picture the fabric of her family with large holes cut out of it. A feeling of loneliness settled over her. *Should I tell Mama and Papa about Miriam's plans? Stop this before it can happen?* But Papa would probably cut Miriam out of the family, just for thinking of leaving, and what good would that do?

"Addie! Please come, child," Mama called from the kitchen. Addie suddenly remembered Uncle Chaim—the bright star in her chest that had been eclipsed by Miriam's talk of running away.

Miriam grabbed Addie's arm. "Addie, please, please, don't speak a word. Promise me. And I have to go out this afternoon, so please?"

Addie nodded, though she didn't want to help Miriam with her plans. She darted for the kitchen, hoping that by leaving Miriam and joining Mama the horrible tearing sensation in her belly would go away.

Mama stood in the kitchen, faced flushed and eyes bright. A pile of unwashed potatoes sat on the wooden table and Addie realized that Mama would need her help and Miriam wouldn't be able to go out. Relief eased the tearing feeling.

"Help me wash and peel these now. Do you have many lessons to do this evening? Tell me what you saw in the streets today." Mama seemed happy and excited. *What does the note say?*

Addie began, telling Mama about the empty streets, the men with drawn-looking faces, the tiny clouds, and the policemen on horses who seemed to lurk on every block. All the while, in the back of her mind, she pictured Miriam trapped in the bedroom with David, safe but miserable.

When Mama went to check on David and Miriam, Addie eyed Mama's special hatbox, which stood out of arm's reach on the high shelf above the jars in the kitchen. Mama must have put Uncle Chaim's letter in the hatbox and would keep it hidden there. She might burn the letter over the stove after Papa left for work tomorrow. *But, no, Mama will risk saving the letter, in case anything happens to Uncle Chaim...to remember him by.* Addie had seen the contents of the hatbox only once, when Mama was rifling through it to find a paper with the stamp of Bohemia on it. There were folded papers, a few old photographs of people Addie didn't recognize, and a collection of hair ribbons that she and Miriam had worn as little girls back in the old country. The silk was frayed and colors fading, but Mama stored them as though they were precious coins to be used in a time of need.

Addie stretched up toward the hatbox, knowing she wouldn't be able to reach but wanting to measure the distance between her fingertips and her uncle's words. *Only about eight inches...eight! Not too far.* The stool Mama used when she chopped and peeled vegetables sat across the kitchen but Addie couldn't move it without making noise. Uncle Chaim felt close by, and she smiled to herself, forgetting the trouble with Miriam for a moment.

Seventeen

ADDIE, STIR the onions so they don't burn," Mama scolded gently.

"Yes, Mama. Sorry, Mama," Addie mumbled.

Papa arrived home just before the evening meal, his cheeks red and twitching with excitement. "We received a new shipment of bowler hats made with a bit of felt that helps hold the shape of the hat better," he exclaimed as the family began to eat.

Addie eyed Mama and Miriam. They both had secrets that Papa must not know about. Thank goodness for his buoyant mood! He seemed too distracted by the new hats to notice Mama and Miriam guarding themselves.

They ate warm cabbage stew and crusty bread and sausages with homemade mustard. Sammy scooted his chair close to Addie's, and she felt glad that the twins were in the apartment so often, even if the reason was David's illness.

"Miriam," Papa said sweetly, using the gentle-kind voice he saved only for her, "tell me about your studies and the extra help you're giving your teacher. Will she write you a letter?"

Miriam almost choked on her sausage. "Yes, Papa. She will." She answered quickly, wiping her mouth carefully with a cloth napkin.

Later, as Addie cleared the table with Miriam and Mama, she tried not to look either of them directly in the eye. Once they were finished, she worked on her lessons at the table and avoided Miriam's heavy stare.

The economy of France relies on exports of ammunition and dairy. 2,274 can be divided by 379 six times.

Addie's eyelids grew heavy over the page and she excused herself from the front room and went to bed. As soon as she lay down and closed her eyes, questions about Miriam began to snake through her brain. *Miriam not a school teacher? Miriam gone to a different state?* Addie had never considered moving away from Chicago and having a different kind of life. *So many people move here to make a better life and yet so many of them are hungry and cold and ill.* Then she thought of Mrs. Raczynski and the women from temple who worked for the Hebrew Ladies Benevolent Society, how they wanted to help poor people in the city. The questions and thoughts kept coming, like the waves on Lake Michigan, until she finally let go into a heavy sleep.

In the morning she rose early, swept the floor in the front room without being asked, and left the apartment for school, before Miriam could beg or scold or confide any more secrets. She walked slowly, noticing the wooden houses and brick buildings. Uncle Ehud often spoke of the great fire that had blazed through Chicago in October 1871, the year before he arrived. Most of the buildings and houses had been wooden then, and a wind from the south had blown fiery sparks into the heart of the city. For the first few years that he'd lived in the city whole blocks remained charred and blackened. Now the Chicago builders used bricks more than wood. Addie remembered the huge torches held by the union protesters. *Would they start another great fire?* A man waiting for a streetcar wore a black bowler hat that looked brand new, like the kind Papa had spoken about at dinner.

Greta hugged Addie excitedly when she arrived at the schoolyard, as though she hadn't seen her in a century. *How much older I feel now*, Addie thought sadly.

"What did you find out about Miriam's boy?" Greta whispered. "Have you seen him at temple?" Her eyes widened before Addie could answer. "He's not a *goy*, is he?" The school bell rang.

"I don't know." Addie shrugged. She hated thinking of the stranger as Miriam's boy. She and Greta walked into the schoolroom, arm in arm, then Addie climbed into her hard wooden desk and set up her inkwell. Miss Green called up the second graders to recite their spelling words. Addie tried to read about the economy of Spain but her mind wandered all over. *Will Mama try to send a note back to Uncle Chaim? And when is Miriam planning to leave? And what's happening to the union organizers who were at the Haymarket?* She looked up from her primer and saw Miss Green leaning over a fourth-grader's lesson book. *Maybe I can ask Miss Green about the unions. She is my teacher, after all.*

At the noon hour most of the children walked home to eat their meals and Greta scuttled off to join her mother at the temple. Addie was tempted to join Greta but decided to wait at her desk to see if Miss Green was staying in the classroom.

"Addie. What is it? Are you feeling unwell again?" Miss Green approached her desk.

"No, ma'am." Addie smiled and felt her face grow red. *It's now or never. I must be brave.* "Miss Green, do you know what happened to the union men since the bombing at the H-Haymarket last week?"

Miss Green sat on the edge of Molly McKeown's empty desk in front of Addie and felt the top and sides of her hair, to make sure her bun was still tight and in order. She tucked a strand of hair back behind her ear and then spoke. "Well, the police are rounding up suspects in the bombing and most of the union activity has stopped for the time being. Unfortunately, I believe this incident has turned most people against the unions." She paused.

Addie wanted her to keep talking but wasn't sure what else to ask without giving away her secrets. "And why...why are there so many poor people in Chicago?"

Miss Green sighed. "Oh, Addie. Such difficult questions you ask. You'll understand more as you grow up. But, as you learn more about the world, you'll see that most places rely on poor people to do hard work. In Chicago, the factories need poor people to operate the machines, otherwise no one would want to do such difficult and dangerous labor. People who work the land in the countryside are also poor, but the poor of Chicago keep the packinghouses running and push the industries forward." Miss Green smiled weakly. "I've probably said enough already."

Ever since seeing the children at work in the sweatshop, and the boy who couldn't be saved by the tourniquet, Addie had thought of the factories and sweatshops as though they were mean bullies. But Papa and Uncle Ehud said the packinghouses, lumberyards, and factories had made Chicago a great city and brought work to thousands of immigrants looking for a better life in America. They spoke with pride about the great Chicago railways that brought live animals in from all over the country and then shipped the butchered meat back to those same places, that brought lumber from other states and then shipped out smooth boards to people who wanted to build houses. Addie imagined the railway like a sea creature with hundreds of tentacles stretching out in all directions. Adults had so many confusing ideas about how the world worked, and the truth always seemed to be lost or hidden just out of sight. *What is the truth? If only the world could be made out of a felt that always held its shape, instead of twisting and changing all the time.*

"M-Miss Green," Addie stammered. "May I ask one more question?"

"Yes, Addie."

"Are the union men the same as the anarchists? Are they all the same?"

Miss Green look relieved. "No, Addie. They aren't. The anarchists are different from the union men...and the socialists and communists are different still. They certainly don't see eye to eye on all matters, but they all believe fiercely in the eight-hour day and most of all want wages and conditions to be fair for workers."

Addie's legs felt cramped from sitting all morning, but she didn't want to get up and end the conversation, just in case Miss Green would say more.

"Addie, where's your dinner pail? Are you going home to eat?" Addie's stomach growled as she realized she only had twenty-five minutes to return home and eat, then get back to school. She slid out from her desk. "Thank you, ma'am." She started to skip away.

"Addie..." Miss Green sounded concerned. "What I say...your parents may not agree with my opinions. But I think it's important to teach children to express their own views. But, as I said, your parents may disagree. And that's okay. That's what democracy is founded on and what we should be proud of as Americans."

Addie imagined Papa storming into Miss Green's classroom and shaking his fist at her. No wonder Miss Green had to be so careful about what she said to her pupils!

"Yes, ma'am. I think I understand. I should go home and eat now. Thank you." Addie scurried out, thinking only of her empty belly.

Eighteen

WITH HIS feet propped up on a stool and his face buried in the *Chicago Tribune*, Papa clucked and sighed dramatically at the news. Addie was sweeping the narrow aisles of the hat shop and stole a quick glance at the paper's headline: A HELLISH DEED—A DYNAMITE BOMB THROWN INTO A CROWD OF POLICEMEN. She took a quiet step closer to Papa, wanting to read more. But the shop bell rang out and interrupted her. Papa rustled the paper closed, folded it and hopped up to greet the customers.

"Welcome, welcome," he called out to an elderly couple, his mood suddenly upbeat and gracious. The man was stooped over, so that his torso hung at a steeply pitched angle above his legs. "Have a seat," Papa offered, pulling his stool over for the man and bowing at the old woman. Papa could be so charming with his customers, kind and sensitive. "We've just received a new shipment of these fine stiff-crowned hats and straw sailors from New York," Papa continued, pointing at the shelves above Addie's head. "Unless, of course, you're here to purchase a hat for the lady." He smiled sweetly and pointed to the display of feathery women's hats on the table.

Addie looked around the small shop and felt a surge of pride. Though the shop was not much bigger than the front room at home and dimly lit, the shelves were neat and organized and the women's hats looked like exotic birds flaunting their hues and shapes. Papa and Uncle Ehud made sure the shop was always dusted and tidy. *So different from the horrible sweatshop,* she thought. *I'm lucky to work here and Papa's lucky he doesn't have a mean boss to order him around.* Addie smiled to herself. *And the boss is lucky not to have Papa to order around!*

Addie continued to sweep while Papa showed the old woman some of the flowerpot hats that stood tall like the roofs on the highest buildings in Chicago. The couple's grandson was getting married next month, and she wanted to look her best, though Addie secretly thought she would look silly wearing such an ornate hat and would do better to buy a pretty new bonnet. The couple spoke to Papa in German, and at first he responded to them in English, but he soon realized they could barely understand him and reluctantly switched to German.

The bell rang out again—this time a cluster of young, boisterous men entered the shop. They crowded the small room with their laughter and movements and tall, lean bodies. They began picking up the new straw boaters, trying them on and teasing each other for looking fancy. Papa and Uncle Ehud had begun making and selling boaters in the shop. A machine for sewing straw had just been invented and made the hats less expensive to weave. Papa eyed them suspiciously, but kept talking to the older couple. Suddenly, Addie recognized Clarence among the group. She almost cried out, then stared down at the little pile of dirt she had swept up and tried to still her mind.

"You won't need any of these leisure-boy hats where you're going next week!" one of the young men joked. "Maybe a cowboy hat instead. A 'Boss of the Plains.'" Addie's stomach lurched. *Next week! Clarence leaves next week? Is Miriam planning to go with him?*

"Well, it's a good time to leave the city, with so many cops sniffing around everywhere," said the tallest young man, who wore red suspenders to hold up his loose-fitting breeches. "Though no one would suspect a baby-faced Mama's boy like you!" He pinched Clarence's cheeks playfully. Addie peeked at

Miriam's beau. His face did look boyish—round yet handsome, with pink cheeks and honey-colored hair. "The cops wouldn't bother with you."

Addie's thoughts shifted to her uncle. *Will Uncle Chaim be picked up by the police?*

"How about this one?" another of the young men asked, pulling a red and white plaid derby down from the shelf.

Now at the counter putting the flowerpot hat in a tall paper box for the old lady, Papa called out to the young men, "Are you just looking today or here to buy?" His voice sounded sharp-cool, and Addie knew he was holding his temper in check for the older couple but might snap at any moment. Addie swept the pile of dirt toward the corner, putting as much distance between herself and Papa as possible.

The shop bell rang out again, and this time Mrs. Raczynski entered, looking winded but determined. She walked right over to Papa and asked to have a quick, private word with him. Papa nodded, which made Addie smile. *Only Mrs. R can interrupt Papa with his customers and get away with it,* she thought. *If only I could be so confident.* After speaking in hushed tones for a moment, Papa called out, "Addie, Mrs. Raczynski needs your help this afternoon. Go on!" And without another glance at Clarence or word from Papa, Addie leaned her broom against the wall, tied on her bonnet, and left the shop arm and arm with Mrs. Raczynski at a brisk clip.

Nineteen

SQUINTING AGAINST the brightness outside, Addie let Mrs. Raczynski lead her along Jefferson Street, heading south. No red line appeared in her head today, as she had no idea where they were going. "Is everything okay? Is Greta hurt?" Addie asked, suddenly worried about her friend.

"Yes, Addie. Greta's fine but she's with her cousins this afternoon and I need help with one of the new immigrant families. Your Papa was good to spare you. I have to admit I was a little vague about what we'd be doing...just some work for the Hebrew Ladies Benevolent Society."

Addie smiled, trying to imagine Papa saying no to Mrs. Raczynski.

"There's a young Russian woman who's just given birth this morning and the midwife must leave to attend to another mother, but the woman has no family *and* has two young children as well as the baby, *and* her husband was picked up by the police last night, so she's quite alone in the world." Mrs. Raczynski pulled her arm out from Addie's and shifted her basket to the other hand. "I have bread and a roast chicken in here, and a bottle of milk for the children. Poor things. They drank milk mixed with poison last month and have been sickly ever since."

Addie nodded and decided to take a chance. "Was her husband a member of one of the unions? Or one of the anarchists involved at the Haymarket bombing?"

Stopping in her tracks, Mrs. Raczynski turned to face Addie and looked surprised, then chuckled. "Aha! I see, your Papa's not the only one in your family who reads the papers. Very good, girl! The eight-hour movement and the Haymarket riot concern all of us and I'm glad you're paying attention." Addie exhaled and her heart quickened. They began walking again. "To answer your question," Mrs. Raczynski continued, "I don't know. The family is Russian and they've only been in Chicago a few months. We'll see if she can even speak German or English and try to find out more. Here, let's take the streetcar down. Their neighborhood is too far for my stiff legs." They waited a few minutes before a streetcar stopped and then climbed aboard. "Do you and your family ride the cars very often, Addie?"

"Sometimes, ma'am," Addie answered. "Just last Sunday our whole family went to Lincoln Park for a picnic."

"Ah! You're a lucky girl, Addie. I hope you realize that. Most immigrant families don't have the time off work, or the streetcar fare, to take such excursions. We take it for granted to have arrived in this country with money in our pockets and the right connections to live well." Addie thought of the workers at the sweatshop and swallowed hard.

They rode the streetcar south for a while, and then got off a block and half from the Russian woman's apartment. Ragged-looking men, and dogs whose ribs jutted through their mange, gathered in the street. One man reached his hand for Mrs. Raczynski's basket but she chided him, "This is for a new mother and her *kinder*. Try the soup kitchen down on Eleventh Street."

To reach the woman's apartment they had to climb five flights of rickety stairs to the very top floor of the building, the air becoming hotter and thicker with every step, and the stench of the nearby stockyards flooding their noses. The stairwell was dark and cramped, and Addie heard a couple shouting in Russian on the second floor. A child wailed from another part of the building and Addie wondered if it was alone.

Tapping softly at the door, Mrs. Raczynski let herself into the apartment, silently beckoning Addie to follow her. The place was tiny—just one room—and so dark that Addie's eyes took a minute to adjust. On the floor sat two small children, a boy and a girl, both wide eyed and quiet. The girl sucked her thumb and held a ragged blanket up to her cheek, while the boy stared listlessly at the basket in Mrs. Raczynski's hand. A soft mewling sound brought Addie's attention to the back corner of the room, where a young woman—who looked no older than Miriam—lay on the floor under a blanket, asleep. A pile of bloody rags lay near her. The mewling came from her side and Addie realized with a start that the sound was her new baby. Mrs. Raczynski knew just what to do. She patted each of the children on the head, found two mugs on a narrow wooden table—the only furniture in the room—and poured some milk for each child.

"Cut up the bread and chicken, Addie. Here you go." She handed Addie the basket and Addie set to work, happy to have a task to stop her from staring at the forlorn family. Meanwhile, Mrs. Raczynski knelt by the woman, gently roused her and picked up the baby. She encouraged the woman to sit up and try to breastfeed. The woman seemed despondent and wouldn't look down at her child, though she did unbutton her nightdress to nurse. Addie's chest ached. *Where is this woman's family to help her? Why is she all alone with these children?* Mrs. Raczynski and the Russian woman spoke quietly in German, and Addie felt relieved that they could at least communicate in a shared language.

Addie brought a plate of bread and chicken over to the children, who had barely sipped their mugs of milk, and asked them in German if they wanted to eat. They looked at her expressionlessly, so she left the plate between them and went back to the table to clean up the crumbs. Mrs. Raczynski brought a tall jar of water and a hunk of bread to the woman, saying in a bright-warm voice, "You need water and food to make milk. So drink up, girl! The best thing for this baby is your milk."

The little boy inched along the floor toward his mother and Mrs. Raczynski broke the hunk of bread into bite sizes so the woman could eat more easily. "Remember," she chatted to the woman, "it's better to have a sparrow in your hand than a dove on the roof. Your children are precious and hold your future, so treasure them beyond all else." Addie marveled at how her very presence made the room feel brighter.

By the time they left an hour later, the woman was sitting up and had invited her older children to come meet their baby brother. The boy and girl had nibbled at the bread but seemed afraid to eat the chicken or drink the milk. Meanwhile, Mrs. Raczynski had collected the bloody rags into her basket, swept the floor, and made sure the family had water and clean blankets.

"Someone from the Society will be along tomorrow to visit and bring more food," Mrs. Raczynski whispered to the woman, as she bent down to kiss the new baby's head. "Remember to keep your strength up with food and water. And sing to the children if you can. That is food for their souls."

Addie felt glad to be leaving, though she also wanted to come back again and find out what the baby had been named and what the children were like when they weren't so shy.

On the ride home Mrs. Raczynski was unusually quiet. Finally, she spoke. "Thank you, Addie, for coming with me today." She sighed heavily. "I found out that poor woman's apartment was searched and her husband was taken in for questioning yesterday and she's received no word at all from him. She has no idea if he'll be back and earn enough to pay for their rent and food. We can only do so much to help."

"Was her husband at Haymarket Square the other night?" Addie asked.

"She kept saying that she didn't know. She seemed fearful and maybe didn't trust me. But, Addie, the police found a substance used to make dynamite..." She paused. "...in the apartment." I'm afraid her husband won't be coming home."

Addie knew that dynamite was used to blast out tunnels, but she also knew that it could be used to make bombs, like the one that had been thrown into the line of policemen at the Haymarket. Mrs. Raczynski closed her eyes and rested her face in her hands until Addie nudged her to let her know that they'd arrived back on Adams Street.

Twenty

O N HER way home from the bakery the next day, Addie stopped by the church to see if Uncle Chaim was there. Mama had sent her off for another loaf of challah with a wink and a kiss on the cheek. They already had enough bread, so Addie guessed that Mama wanted her to see about Uncle Chaim. She skipped along Halsted Street, her legs racing along like a runaway horse.

Addie turned the corner of Adams Street and scanned the scaffolding but saw no sign of Uncle Chaim. She craned her neck, hoping that passersby would only think she was interested in the church construction. Just as she'd decided to give up and go home, she heard the familiar sound, "Pssst! Addie!" Her heart leapt, though she knew to be careful and not run right to him. She looked around to see who was nearby—an old woman, bent and hobbling across the street, and two men deep in conversation strolling by. She slipped behind the scaffolding and whispered, "Oh, Uncle Chaim! I'm so glad to see you again!" Mama had given her several boiled potatoes and some dried meat in a small sack to give to him, in case he was at the church again. The potatoes were two days old now, but Addie knew he'd eat anything Mama sent along.

"Here!" She thrust the sack into his hands. Uncle Chaim's face looked sad and frightened. "What is it, Uncle? Is something the matter?"

"Oh, Addie!" Uncle Chaim grabbed a clump of his curly hair. "One of my comrades is here, behind the church, and he's in terrible pain. I don't know what to do for him." He stopped speaking to compose himself. "He screams in his sleep and I'm afraid he'll attract the attention of a policeman. We must get out of the city, in case we're caught and accused of being part of the bombing, but he's in so much pain that he can barely move."

Addie felt relieved that Uncle Chaim was okay, but his words "get out of the city" rang in her ears. "What happened to him?" she asked.

"He was trying to escape the other night at the Haymarket. We were in a crowd and the police were firing on us, and he tried to climb onto a wagon, but got caught in a tangle of men and his arm twisted before he could let go."

Addie shuddered, memories of the frantic night at Haymarket Square swarming her like flies on a dung heap.

"The problem is…Michael's a typesetter for a labor newspaper. His fingers are stained with ink and the police will surely suspect him of printing flyers for the protesters if they see that and then find out where he works." Uncle Chaim began pacing. "If only I could bring him to a doctor, but I'm afraid of being caught. Addie, the police aren't concerned with *who* they catch, only that they find someone to blame for the bombs."

Addie nodded, though she understood very little. "May I see him?" she asked in a quiet voice. She wasn't sure that she wanted to see him but Uncle Chaim seemed so alone and frightened, and she longed to help if she could. She followed her uncle toward a moaning sound behind the church. A huddled figure in a dark gray overcoat lay against the wall.

"Michael," Uncle Chaim called softly to him. "I've brought my niece Addie to see you. Don't be afraid."

The man didn't look up. He continued moaning softly and Addie forced herself to look at him. She searched his body for a missing part, something horribly disfigured or bloody, but could find nothing wrong. Uncle Chaim nodded to Addie, as if he understood what she was looking for. "Michael, I'd like to show her your arm. May I lift your coat?"

Addie realized that one of the sleeves of his overcoat was flat with nothing in it. The man grunted and for a moment his moaning stopped. Uncle Chaim beckoned for Addie to come crouch near the man. She couldn't see his face and had no idea how old he was or even the color of his hair. His head hung down and he had on a soft cap, which was pulled low over his forehead. Uncle Chaim carefully pulled back his coat, and revealed Michael's right arm hanging lifeless. Addie gasped. A large, unnatural looking bump stood out from the front of his shoulder. The arm looked like it no longer belonged to Michael. Addie took a step back, wanting to look away, but knew he desperately needed help. He began moaning again, and Uncle Chaim and Addie retreated back to the side of the building.

Addie felt shaken and helpless. *What can I possibly do to help?* She still didn't understand anarchism or what would help the striking workers. She didn't know how to bring peace between Papa and Uncle Chaim, or how to get Michael safely out of Chicago. She was just a young girl in a huge, bewildering city. Her mind raced over all the events of the past two weeks, desperate for an answer, something to hold onto. *What can I do? What can I possibly do?* And then she felt a familiar sense of hope and vibrancy in her chest and her mind returned to Dr. Goldstein. *He said I could be a nurse... or a doctor. A lady doctor. An Ärztin. He asked me to keep a secret from Papa.* She had understood how the tourniquet worked and could stomach seeing blood if it meant helping. And Dr. Goldstein knew her better since David had gotten sick and would surely help her. She looked at her uncle, wanting to share the shred of hope she had found but also afraid of sounding foolish.

"Perhaps...perhaps I could go to Dr. Goldstein and get help, or find out what to do..." Her voice trailed off as she began to doubt herself.

"No, no, Addie." Uncle Chaim shook his head. "We can't ask Dr. Goldstein to come. We would put him in danger of being arrested for conspiring with the protesters."

Her mind turned over and over, searching for a way. "*I could go to Dr. Goldstein and tell him what I've seen and find out what he recommends. It's the only hope...if Michael can't go to a doctor himself.*"

Uncle Chaim sat for a moment. He pulled out a pencil and scrap of paper and scratched out a quick note. "Addie, give this to your mother and, if you can, visit Dr. Goldstein. But only if it doesn't put you in danger. Please be careful. I could never forgive myself if something bad came of this," he said, his voice scared-sad.

Before he could change his mind, Addie gave him a quick hug and ran off. She knew Papa would not leave the hat shop in the middle of the day, but she still felt afraid of crossing his path. A man limping slowly across the street wore a shabby-looking bowler hat. Addie wondered if he'd brought it from the old country or purchased it in Chicago, or perhaps New York on his way here. The man's left shoulder slumped forward as if hiding something. Addie forced herself to stop staring at him. She hurried to pass him and focused on getting to Dr. Goldstein's. *It'll be easy enough to avoid Papa this time of day.* She pictured a map of the neighborhood and drew the red line from the church to the doctor's house. The line had four right angles that zigzagged across the city. The closest the red line got to the hat shop was two whole blocks. *Plenty of buffer,* Addie thought.

As she ran, she thought of Papa talking to the people who ambled along the street in front of his shop, looking for nothing in particular. "Come in, friend!" he always called cheerfully. He had adopted the relaxed American attitude, to avoid seeming pushy or over eager. Addie felt a stab of shame at deceiving Papa. *He tries to control us all but really he just wants us to be safe. Just like me, he wants our family to be whole.* Mama teased that the long years of separation had turned him into a clucking hen, never at rest until all the chicks were corralled into a safe corner. Addie pushed the image from her mind and focused on the cobblestones beneath her feet.

Suddenly, she remembered the note. She thrust her right hand into her pocket and felt for the slippery paper from Uncle Chaim. *Phew!* The note was there, folded and tucked safely away. Rounding Clinton Street, Addie saw a man with his young family, six children in all, walking slowly along the sidewalk looking carefully at each building. He looked lost and the children hung onto one another, as if to a life raft. Their clothes looked worn, though patched and sewn with care. Addie was curious if they were German and where their mother was.

Her mind shifted back to Uncle Chaim. *Is he part of the conspiracy to hurt the Chicago policemen?* It was almost too much to think about. *Sweet, playful Uncle Chaim. How could it be?* Papa's angry words and Mama's pleading echoed through Addie's head. A knot tightened in her stomach. She couldn't imagine life without Uncle Chaim, and yet the brick wall Papa had erected felt impossible to climb over or knock down. *If only the wall were made of wood, and not brick, we could burn it down,* Addie thought, then shook her head. *I'm thinking like a crazy person now!*

Twenty-One

THE SUN raced across the sky as Addie ran down Jackson Street. Some of the factories must have let workers go for the day, as the sidewalks were crowded with men who reeked of tar and blood and sweat. Addie could not get the picture of Uncle Chaim's friend with his slackened arm out of her head. And then she imagined how Dr. Goldstein's face might look after she asked him for help. *What have I gotten myself into?* Her legs moved like the spokes of a bicycle wheel, smooth and blurred by speed. She turned onto Clinton and made her way to the doctor's house without a plan of what she would say. *I need to move quickly now, before I lose my nerve.* She knocked on the door, the raps sounding hollow and empty. Before she could catch her breath, the door swung open and Dr. Goldstein stood on the threshold.

"Addie. Hello! Has David taken a turn for the worse?"

Addie's chest tightened and her tongue stuck to the roof of her mouth.

"Ah...no, Doctor. Well, I don't know, sir, how David is. I haven't been home since earlier today...when he was resting," Addie sputtered.

"Well, what is it then, child? I'm on my way to an appointment."

"You see, sir," she stammered, unsure of how to begin. "It's just that..."

"Addie, is something wrong?" Dr. Goldstein looked concerned.

Addie's thoughts began to splinter in different directions.

Does Dr. Goldstein support the union men? Is it safe to tell him the whole truth? Does he care about politics, or only about helping sick and injured people? What if he's like Papa and hates the unions and blames them for the city's problems? What if he tells Papa?

Addie looked at Dr. Goldstein and began slowly, hoping that she'd be able to read his face as she spoke and then form her words based on his reactions.

"You see, my Uncle Chaim went missing...only I just found him, but he's had an accident...he's hiding from...he's hiding... but needs help." In a split second she'd decided to pretend that Uncle Chaim was the injured one, and not Michael, a stranger. She prayed that Dr. Goldstein would not insist on seeing her uncle himself but, instead, would tell her how to help him. She realized too late that the lie might make things more complicated.

Dr. Goldstein took hold of her elbow. "Come in, child," he said in a hushed voice. By his gentle but urgent tone, Addie knew he would help. Her heart gushed with relief and gratitude. But then she felt treacherous for not telling the whole truth.

Dr. Goldstein led her into the parlor and pointed to a chair she could sit on. "Now, tell me everything. Where's your uncle? How bad is his injury?"

Addie closed her eyes and tried to think. *How much can I say? I've trapped myself inside a half-lie.* "I met him in the streets by chance. I haven't seen him since he and Papa fought last week." Addie sighed. "The arm, it...it...hangs like so." She splayed her arm out and waved it back and forth, as though it was unhinged from her shoulder. "And there's a big lump here." She pointed to the front of her shoulder. "Do you think a tourniquet would help it?"

The doctor thought for a moment. "Is there blood? An open wound?"

Addie rubbed her hands together, suddenly feeling cold and wishing she had a shawl to pull around her shoulders. She wanted to hide part of herself from the doctor, to carve away more time to think and tease out the lies from the truth. She thought of

Mama's yarn when it became tangled and needed a pair of patient hands to unfurl it from itself. *Why didn't I puzzle this out better?*

"No, sir. I didn't see any blood, though there might have been some."

"Addie." Dr. Goldstein looked at her hard. "I'm guessing he won't come in here to see me himself. I won't ask you to betray your uncle. But he'll struggle his whole life with only one working arm. Can you remember anything else about how his arm looked?"

Addie swallowed. *Why didn't I pay better attention to Michael's arm while I had the chance?* Behind the church she'd wanted to blot the image of his lifeless arm and the grotesque lump from her mind, but now she desperately needed to see it all. She closed her eyes to recall the scene more clearly. "His hand was white, almost blue really, and it hung as though not properly attached to the rest of him. I didn't see any blood through his shirt, but he looked to be in terrible pain."

Dr. Goldstein scratched his whiskered chin and cocked his head to one side. "It sounds as though he's dislocated his shoulder, Addie," he explained. "Are you quite sure your uncle won't see me himself? That would be best."

Addie swallowed and answered, "No, sir," hoping she didn't sound rude or ungrateful. Dr. Goldstein strode across the room to a little desk in the corner and took out a piece of paper. He dipped his pen into an inkwell and scribbled onto the paper for a few minutes. *Is he writing a note to Uncle Chaim?* Addie felt a pang of relief. *Perhaps delivering the note will be my only responsibility.* Dr. Goldstein stretched the paper out in front of her.

"Look here." The paper showed a rough sketch of the bones in the shoulder joint.

"This is the ball and socket of the shoulder. The ball," he pointed, "fits into the shallow socket...here. Whatever your uncle was doing caused them to separate." He paused and Addie studied the paper closely, so that she wouldn't have to look him in the eye. "You'll need to push them back together so that the arm can move properly. You can do that with a leveraging technique."

Addie squinted at the paper and felt a sense of dread pooling down into her belly.

"Listen carefully, Addie. You must rotate the forearm like so, until he feels some pressure. You'll need help. Find someone, anyone, to help you." Dr. Goldstein held her forearm and demonstrated twisting it outwards until it would go no further. "Then you must lift it up and forward as far as possible, and finally thrust and twist it back into the ball." He sighed. "Can you imagine that, Addie? You won't be able to see much, but think of the diagram of the ball and socket. You must find someone to help you."

Addie nodded but her stomach burned with doubt and fear. She closed her eyes and asked Dr. Goldstein to repeat the directions so she could try to see it all in her mind's eye.

After describing the procedure in finer detail, he asked, "Tell me, Addie. Is he alone?" His voice sounded worried-warm.

How can I answer Dr. Goldstein directly, while still keeping enough of the truth hidden? "No, sir. There'll be someone to help." She bowed her head, hoping to be excused and on her way back to her uncle. The scrap of paper and the brief instructions seemed too meager, but lying made her anxious, and she desperately wanted to leave.

"Remember to hold the shoulder steady and then twist the arm to the right. You should hear a clicking sound. He'll be in quite a bit of pain but you must continue until you hear the clicking." Addie nodded and bowed her head again. "Wait, Addie, one more thing." He walked to a low cabinet made of dark wood near his desk. She bristled with impatience and dread. *Why does he keep holding me up?* He pulled out a small bottle of alcohol and handed it to her. *Whiskey?* "He might need this. The procedure can be very, very painful and it'll go more smoothly if he drinks some of this."

Addie placed the bottle and piece of paper in her right pocket, a cousin to the note from Uncle Chaim, which was hidden in her left pocket. "Thank you, sir," she said quietly. "Our family is very much obliged to you." She looked at the doctor now, wondering if he understood that Papa could not know about this visit.

"Yes," he replied. "Our ties go back to the old country. We're practically family. Come now." He smiled at Addie but his eyes looked sad and tired. "And maybe someday you'll become a doctor after all." He walked Addie to the front door and she slipped out of the house without another word. Once outside, she ran like the wind off the lake. She feared the task ahead and the unavoidable fact that it would make her late getting home, to Papa's sure fury. *No time to linger on the future beyond today,* she thought, as she tucked the doctor's final words away, to ponder and relish another time.

Twenty-Two

SMOKE FROM a kitchen fire filled Addie's nose as she raced back to the church. Her legs felt tired and heavy from running and her throat burned from the smoke, but she kept moving quickly. *I must get home before dark.* The sun sank deeper in the western sky, a warning to hurry up. *How long will this take?* She arrived at the church and found Uncle Chaim leaning over Michael, tipping liquid from a small tin flask into his mouth. *Good,* she thought, *Uncle Chaim is already giving him something to ease the pain.*

"Addie!" Uncle Chaim cried when he looked up. "You're back so soon. What happened?" Her hands shook as she pulled the paper from her pocket and explained to him about the doctor's diagnosis and the procedure for setting Michael's arm right.

"I've seen something like this before, at a farm back in Germany," Uncle Chaim said as he studied the paper. "An ox stepped into a hornet's nest while our neighbor was plowing his field, and the animal went wild and pulled the man's arm out of its socket as he fled. I believe his arm was all right in the end, but it hung like this until the doctor came and fixed it."

Uncle Chaim tussled Addie's hair and smiled. For a moment he seemed like his old self, cheerful and twinkly. "Come, now, let's try it." He knelt beside Michael, who looked up with the dark, sad eyes of a wounded animal, and Addie got a good look at him for the first time. His beard and mustache were well groomed, and his face looked kind, though frightened.

"There now," Uncle Chaim crooned. "Addie and I'll try to put your arm back in place. Just grit your teeth together and it should be over in a moment."

Michael squeezed his eyes shut, and his face closed up on itself, like sea creatures Addie had read about in school. She heard two men shouting at each other on the street in front of the church. The yelling, which sounded like it was in Italian, got louder and meaner. Addie's heart skipped a beat. *Will they attract policemen or crowds to the front of the church?*

Uncle Chaim looked worried, too, and began to hurry. He pulled a handkerchief from his pocket and handed it to Addie. "You must cover his mouth with this and then hold the back of his head so that he can't pull away from you. Don't be afraid."

Addie took the handkerchief and her hands began to shake again. Michael's hair felt oily and slick in her left hand, and the thick hairs of his beard tickled the edges of her right palm. The shouting men had moved further down the block and other voices joined in. *Perhaps they'll help settle the argument and the danger will pass.*

Meanwhile, Uncle Chaim held Michael's shoulder down with one hand and gripped his forearm with the other. He looked at Addie and counted softly to three in German, "*Eins, zwei, drei!*" As Uncle Chaim twisted and thrust—just as Dr. Goldstein had directed—Michael, in agony, tried to sit up. His mouth widened so that the whole handkerchief fell into it and Addie felt his cool lips and saliva against her fingers. Her stomach heaved. *Michael must stay quiet so that we're not caught.*

Addie heard a loud clicking sound and then Michael's body went limp. He started moaning and rocking himself and, though she could not hear distinct words, he seemed to be praying. Uncle Chaim's face was red from the effort, and the veins in his neck bulged, but he continued to hold the arm, now delicately, in his two large hands. He seemed afraid to let go, as if Michael's arm might crumble into dust or disappear altogether if he dropped it.

Ever so carefully, Uncle Chaim pulled away until the arm lay against Michael's chest. Addie couldn't tell if his arm was back in place, as it was curled up like a sleeping cat. Michael was quiet, almost peaceful. Addie's chest felt tight and she longed to stay with her uncle and wait to see if Michael was better. But the sun, now hidden by buildings, cautioned her to rush home. "Uncle, I need to go. Papa'll be angry when I come in so late, but I promise to come again as soon as I can."

"Addie," Uncle Chaim said quietly and took both her hands. "Thank you. You've been very brave. Remember to stand up straight, show the world your true height." His voice sounded proud-strained. He stopped then, remembering something. "Do you still have the note for your Mama?" Addie felt for the note in her pocket and nodded. The note was a bit of her uncle that she could keep with her on her way home. "Give her a kiss for me." His eyes looked wet. "Oh, how I miss you all."

Addie knew she must run quickly, like the steam trains that roared in from the East. She gave her uncle a hug and he kissed the top of her head lightly and then she was gone. The way between the apartment and the church was so familiar now that she didn't even notice the red line in her head, pulsing with warning and urgency. Instead, she was aware of night falling and the light disappearing like water through her hands.

Twenty-Three

DDIE HESITATED on the steps of their building and touched Uncle Chaim's note, folded and folded again in her pocket. Then she opened the door to let herself in, with her shoulders hunched forward. Taking a deep breath, she thought of Uncle Chaim's words. So, she stood up tree-tall, felt the knobs in the middle of her spine unfurl and lengthen, and walked into the apartment. Papa was staring out the window onto the street with an expression of disgust on his lips. Much to her surprise, he grunted and didn't shift his gaze. *I must give Mama the note before he notices me.* Miriam stood at the washbasin in the kitchen, peeling potatoes and humming an old German song. Addie smiled at Mama.

"I stopped by the church again to see how the renovation is coming." Addie relished having her sweet secret with Mama, something only the two of them shared.

Mama kept her eyes on Addie but spoke to Miriam. "Miriam, please see if David needs anything."

Instead of protesting, as Addie expected, Miriam nodded dreamily, laid the paring knife by the potatoes and left the kitchen. Mama, perched at the edge of a stool washing plates, looked up at Addie with longing and anxiety. Addie handed her the note, though she hated to part with it. Mama dried her hands on her apron and began to unfold it carefully.

Just as she'd opened the paper fully, Papa stormed into the

kitchen. He pounced on Mama, grabbed the note from her hand and stood back to read it. He held the sheet out in front of him like a piece of trash. His hands shook with rage, making the paper shudder and rasp. He glared at Mama, then turned to Addie.

"You!" He pointed at her with his index finger. "How dare you? You…you…strange and terrible child."

She froze, her legs and arms tingling in alarm. She looked down and studied the wooden floor, the straight lines of the pine planks and the flat, round heads of the nails. She waited for a blow to her head or shouting to explode in her ears. She thought of the small window behind her. *Perhaps I can escape and fly like a bird to the street below.*

Papa's hand slapped her ear, sending a shock through her temples and neck. Her cheek stung, but she managed to contain the scream that rose in her throat.

"Josef, no!" Mama cried. "It's my fault. Addie only followed my directions." Mama was pulling on Papa's sleeve. He grabbed her by the shoulders. Addie had never seen Papa raise a hand against Mama and feared the worst.

Mama looked strong and fearless in Papa's grasp. Her eyes were steely, as though Papa could do nothing more to hurt her. "Josef, listen to me. Chaim is living on the streets with very little to eat and nowhere to sleep at night. You must understand, he's my blood and I will not turn my back on him."

Very little to eat? No place to sleep? Addie realized that Uncle Chaim was telling Mama more in his notes than she knew from seeing him at the church.

Papa shook Mama and spat on the floor. "Chaim and the other anarchists are spoiling all that we have here. Already the American customers come into our shop less. They no longer trust immigrants."

"Josef, no. He's just that small boy you remember from the farm. Remember? Remember? We are family."

Addie tried to imagine Uncle Chaim as a small boy, but could only see him as a bear-man, tall and hulking with his soft beard and twinkling eyes.

"I don't want workers causing trouble with the anarchists and socialists and communists—and turning the city violent— anywhere near my house or with my family," Papa shouted in his loud-terrible voice. "Chaim has always been a troublemaker and this is no different."

Mama's eyes filled with tears and the crease in her forehead began to throb.

"I forbid you to help your brother again," Papa declared. Then, suddenly, he covered his face with his hands and began to sob.

Mama ran to him and stood next to him, though she didn't touch him. "Josef, what is it? Are you unwell?"

Papa shook his head. His voice was softer now, almost a whisper. "Perhaps we should not have brought the children here. Look at them. Moshe interested in the law and turning his back on the family business. And Addie sneaking around on the streets with no shame. I hardly know the girl." His voice was now full of regret. "This city is too dangerous for our children. They no longer respect the family and then what good is any of it?"

Mama said nothing. Addie's ear still blazed where Papa had struck it. As much as she hated Papa in that moment, she wished that Mama would reach for him and touch his back or arm to reassure him. Papa continued his quiet rant. "What kind of place is this to raise children anyway, with so much unrest?" His eyes filled with tears.

Suddenly, Miriam called out from the back room. "Mama, Papa, come quickly!"

Papa looked up as though he'd just been woken from a vivid dream. He noticed Addie slinking near the door and his face filled with color. He stood up abruptly and pointed his finger at her. The crumpled man was gone. "Don't you try to sneak out of here again." Tiny beads of spit flew from his mouth as he spoke. "I'll throw you out of this family if I find out that you're running off to see your uncle again."

Addie's legs began to shake.

"Papa, Mama, please come now!" Miriam's voice sounded high and strained.

Mama startled at Miriam's voice. She grabbed Papa by the elbow and pushed him out of the kitchen. Addie felt frozen inside. Papa's words had turned her to stone. But Miriam's voice was urgent and concern overcame her. She darted to the back room, where David lay on the cot looking white and shivering uncontrollably. Miriam knelt beside him, wrapping a wool blanket around him, as Mama bent over to feel his forehead. David's eyes were closed but he moved his head from side to side and groaned in discomfort. His breath came hard and fast. Addie longed to be invisible, to be with her family but not draw any attention to herself, especially from Papa.

"He's burning with fever," Mama whispered. "Josef, Addie should get Ehud from the shop. Perhaps we should send for the doctor."

Papa looked at Addie, as though considering his options, and then a snarl overtook his face. "Where's Moshe?" he almost yelled. "Moshe must get the doctor." *Papa's dismissing me from the family, my usefulness is frayed beyond repair.*

"Shhhhhh," Miriam chided. "David needs rest."

Papa wrung his hands. "I'll get Ehud and take over at the shop and he can decide what to do. I don't know how to manage this family anymore!" He stormed past Addie and slammed the front door behind him. Mama squeezed out a cool cloth and applied it to David's forehead. Addie felt exhausted, as though she were the cloth that had just been twisted and pulled. David's breath was fast and shallow, thin like a whisper.

As soon as Papa left, Mama turned to Addie. "Please go get the doctor. I fear this is the end."

Twenty-Four

DDIE BURST into the apartment with Dr. Goldstein half a staircase behind her. He panted heavily on the steps, stopped for a moment and then resumed the climb.

Widow Adler must have heard the racket of their entry, as she hobbled to the edge of the railing on the second floor. Seeing the doctor, she called out, "Oh, my! Has the boy taken a turn for the worse?" Without waiting for an answer, she continued, "Let me know if I can be of assistance, Doctor."

Dr. Goldstein could only nod as he panted and sucked in air. He continued mounting the last of the stairs.

Addie heard the sound of muffled wailing as she entered the apartment. Moshe, Miriam, and Sammy crowded the entryway to the back bedroom. Miriam's arms were draped around Sammy and Moshe leaned against the threshold, his head bowed. Addie's stomach fell out from under her. The wails were coming from Mama. The sound of David's coughing and wheezing were gone, like a panel missing from Mama's old quilt. *Is he suddenly well? Is that why his coughing has finally stopped?* But Mama's cries... *No. We're too late.* A sob caught in Addie's throat. Papa and Uncle Ehud were reciting a Hebrew prayer, and Addie recognized the words, *Barukh atah Adonai, Eloheinu melekh ha'olam, dayan ha-emet*—the traditional Jewish blessing spoken at the time of someone's death. Addie wanted to run down the stairs and make time move backward. If only she could run fast enough, her life would become a blur with no clear forms, no endings, no beginnings.

Dr. Goldstein called out, "Ehud, Josef, Sara." His voice sounded smooth and heavy, like a river stone. He pushed past Moshe, Miriam, and Sammy.

Moshe twisted around and saw Addie. His eyes were red and he shook his head, and then reached out to her. "Oh, Addie. He stopped breathing a few minutes ago. He's gone." Moshe's voice broke and he began to weep silently. Addie rested her hand on his arm. She'd never seen Moshe cry before. She felt frozen again, her chest aching from what felt like a hard and bitter frost. *How could David have slipped away from us? Where is his soul now? Is he really gone?*

Miriam and Sammy followed Dr. Goldstein and stood huddled around the cot with the others. Dr. Goldstein spoke to Mama and Papa and Uncle Ehud quietly. Mama's wailing had stopped, and now she rocked back and forth, as though putting a baby to sleep. Uncle Ehud sat beside David, tenderly stroking his son's face. Then he addressed Sammy. "Son, can you close your brother's mouth and cover him with this sheet?" Addie remembered the tradition from when Auntie Rebecca had died. The youngest family member who was able to would shut the eyes and mouth of the dead person and cover their body with a sheet. Sammy and David and Addie had been too young at the time, so Miriam had stoically covered her aunt's body. Sammy nodded and Mama brought him a starched white sheet to cover his brother. Addie shut her eyes and leaned against Moshe, not sure she could stand on her own anymore. Once David was covered, the adults carefully moved him to the floor and Mama lit candles near his head.

Dr. Goldstein removed the stethoscope from around his neck. "May his soul rest in peace now." He stood up. "David fought hard. He held on longer than most." He put his hand on Uncle Ehud's shoulder. "Please call on me if anyone else in the family falls ill."

Mama let out a single sob. Dr. Goldstein leaving meant that there was truly no help left for David. But then she stopped crying, wiped her hands on her dress, and stood up. *How can she stop the tears, like turning off a faucet, and just carry on?* Addie stood numbly watching the scene, unable to hear anything but blood pulsing in her ears, *whoosh, whoosh, whoosh,* and watching as Mama reached into her dress pocket and pulled out her coin purse to pay the doctor.

"Sara, no. Save the money for the undertaker. I did nothing here today." His voice was heavy-soft.

Mama's eyes filled with tears.

"Your kindness is a great solace to us," Papa said. He sounded empty and hollow, the usual irritation in his voice gone. He stood and led the doctor into the hall, where they spoke quietly. Addie inched toward the door, hoping to hear bits of their conversation. With Uncle Chaim on the run and now David dead, Addie needed to know what was coming next. *Will Sammy get sick now? Will Uncle Ehud die of a broken heart? Has Mama exposed herself to sickness while taking care of David?*

From the edge of the door, Addie heard Dr. Goldstein instruct Papa. "Call the undertaker first thing in the morning, then alert the temple and they'll make arrangements for a burial." He paused. "Make sure Ehud eats and sleeps. And watch Sammy closely. I'm not far away, if you need me. The family must stay together during these times." Addie thought of Uncle Chaim, lurking in a dark alley somewhere, hungry and afraid and waiting for news of a police search. *He should be with us now. Not alone and frightened for his life.*

Addie and her family spent the whole night sitting in the back bedroom near David, Mama weeping and Uncle Ehud shaking his head and pulling his beard. Addie felt numb and cold, and she eventually nodded off to sleep. She woke to morning light streaming in the back room and Papa peering down at her with his beetle brown eyes and great eyebrows.

"Can you go find the undertaker now? The weather is getting warm and we must put David's body to rest as soon as possible." Papa sounded far away, as if from a dream, but he'd forgiven Addie enough to send her out again.

She nodded, remembering when she and Papa had gone to get the undertaker after Aunt Rebecca died. She felt a familiar surge of energy at the thought of leaving the apartment. The task would save her from drowning under the weight of David's death, from being pulled down into a dark hold. It was a chance to stretch her legs on the streets, to observe the vile, gray city with so many people and buildings and smells, to lose herself for a time. Part of her longed to bury her head in Mama's lap and weep for David, but not just yet. *I'll go and find the undertaker for Papa and then face this terrible truth a bit later.*

She ran down the apartment steps. *How will we go on without David? How will Uncle Ehud survive this?* The thought of Sammy, a single knitting needle without its pair, made her choke. *Little Sammy, who'd lost his mother five years ago to typhoid, and now this.* Addie moved as fast as she could, hoping that maybe she could outrun the grim faces of her family and perhaps death itself. She turned down Adams Street, toward the river and the undertaker's shop. The red line pulsed and swirled, moving about in her mind's eye before she could focus enough to orient herself. Lost and yet unwilling to stop, she kept going toward the river and hoped her head would clear by the time she reached it.

Running behind a carriage, she tried to keep pace with the horse and use the space behind it as her path. She looked up and saw the entrance to an alley that would spit her out down by the docks and provide her a quieter passage. Suddenly, she remembered the date—May 9th. *David died on May the eighth. Eight again! Is it a cursed number? A number of change? Perhaps a number that tears family into little bits of useless rags?*

Her head throbbed and tears streaked her cheeks, but she didn't even bother to wipe her face. Though no one seemed to notice her, she suddenly longed for privacy. She ran across the street, aiming for the alley. Thinking of David's pale body, still warm from the life that had left it only hours before, she desperately wanted to let all of the sadness pour out from her. Pour down to the river and into the lake that spanned the eastern horizon like a great ocean. And then suddenly, everything went black, and Addie collapsed in a heap in the alley.

Twenty-Five

ADDIE AWOKE to find herself cradled in Papa's arms. He was standing in the alley panting. Her knees stung and her left leg throbbed but she was mostly aware of Papa—how he smelled of cigar smoke and damp wool and sweat, and how his breath was ragged, like a steam train slowing into the station. His face looked as if it had caved in on itself. His cheeks hung low and his jaw sunk down toward his collar. Seeing her eyes open, he tried to speak, but coughed instead. She couldn't remember ever being so near Papa and looked away from him to avoid too much closeness.

"Addie." His voice was a tender growl. "We'll go home now. Moshe has gone to get the undertaker. You must rest." Addie nodded and shifted uncomfortably in his arms. "Put your arms around my neck so I can hold onto you better," he said gently and moved his arm lower on her back to be able to carry her more easily.

Addie held her breath, afraid that she was too much for Papa and then asked quietly, "But, Papa, how did you know where to find me?" She looked around at the narrow alley darkened by the shadows of surrounding buildings. It felt like a lonely, forgotten place, and she rested her head against Papa for comfort.

Papa cleared his throat. "The widow told us. She saw you leaving and said you weren't fit to be out alone, that your eyes were filled with tears and you couldn't possibly see clearly. She followed you out and saw you collapse and came up all the stairs to tell us." Papa started slowly walking down the block toward the apartment, now huffing and puffing. "She didn't want us to lose two children in the same week." His voice cracked.

The Widow Adler out on the street? Following me and making sure I was all right? She could hardly picture it. The widow seemed so frail. Addie's throat tightened as she thought of the old woman risking her safety to protect Addie. She'd always dreaded the widow's constant presence in their neighborhood, her comments and warnings, the scowl on her face. *She's been watching out for me all along.*

"Papa, I could try to walk. I don't want to strain your back," Addie said, not wanting to hurt Papa's feelings but uncomfortable and cramped in his tight embrace. *So strange that Papa won't usually so much as pat my shoulder and now he's holding me so close to him.*

"No, no, Addie. I have you now." His voice sounded tender-sad. "The widow's right. She scolded me for not taking better care of you, for relying on you too much, sending you out on so many errands and not paying enough attention." He squeezed Addie to his chest, and she could hear his lungs filling with air and the sound of his heart thumping. His whiskers tickled the top of her head and she thought, *He does love me. Only the love looks a little different.*

Addie lay on her bed, humming the German lullaby Mama used to sing to David. A lone tear slid down her cheek and she pushed her head down into the pillow. Her leg still throbbed from falling down suddenly in the alley, but the pain was a kind distraction from David's absence. Papa, Mama, Sammy, and Uncle Ehud had gone to the temple to make arrangements for David's burial. Addie could hear Miriam and Moshe talking in the front room and felt a stab of loneliness. She slid off the bed and shuffled down the hall to find Miriam sitting at the table and Moshe standing by the window looking down on the street.

"Addie, sit down. Mama says you should be resting as much as possible," Miriam said. She sounded so much like Mama, but not as kind. Addie obliged her and sat down. Moshe opened the window and leaned out. A man and woman were shouting at each other on the street. By the thick drawl of the man's voice Addie guessed he was drunk. A breeze blew reluctantly into the front room, as though not sure it wanted to enter into such a sad household. Miriam's eyes were red and puffy.

"Addie," she said in her bossy-loud voice, "Moshe and I were discussing his future plans. Can you keep a secret?"

Addie felt irritated. *Haven't I kept C-L-A-R-E-N-C-E a secret these past weeks? Does she really think I'm such a baby still?* But she bit her tongue and nodded.

"In that case…" Miriam's voice began to rise as she turned back to Moshe. "…aren't you worried about breaking Papa's heart? He's expecting you to take over the shop. Now with David gone…" Her voice trailed off and a whirlpool pulled Addie's belly down and inward. Her cheeks began to flame with confusion and anger. *How can Miriam speak of Moshe breaking Papa's heart when she has plans to move to a claim in Dakota Territory?* Angry words pushed themselves up and out of her mouth before she could think clearly.

"But what about you, Miriam? Aren't you leaving us, as well? How can you blame Moshe for anything, when you plan to move to Dakota Territory?" Anger gave way to grief and Addie began to wail uncontrollably and without any shred of care. The world as she knew it was coming apart, the seams unwinding before her very eyes. Moshe rushed over and knelt beside her. She felt hot and sticky, yet better for crying like this, as though something deep inside her had finally broken free and she no longer had to be silent.

"I think she's sick, Moshe. I don't know what she's talking about."

Moshe, who had his hand on Addie's shoulder and was looking at her with concern, sneered at Miriam. "You don't think I know about you and that boy? Oh, Miriam! Do you think I was born yesterday?"

Miriam took a step back. Addie stopped crying and wiped her tears with her hands. Miriam turned to get a handkerchief, moving slowly to give herself time to think of how to respond. The clock ticked in the silence. Miriam's eyes darted as she wiped Addie's tears. "Well, I've decided not to leave, anyway. I'll stay in this horrible place until I can walk out the door with my head held high." Her voice caught on a snag as she spoke, but she didn't cry. "Clarence has already left for Dakota and he'll send for me when I'm finished with school," she said resolutely.

Addie took a deep breath and pondered the meaning of Miriam's words. Miriam had two more years before she would complete school, which seemed like a very long time. But, if she left in good standing with Papa she could write letters freely and perhaps even come home to visit. Most people didn't see their relatives once they moved west, or very rarely, but at least they could write letters back and forth.

Addie hiccupped and smiled in spite of herself.

"Oh, Addie," Miriam said, her voice sounding warm, like soft wool. She almost sounded as sweet as Mama. "Don't cry anymore. We've had enough tears today to last us a lifetime." She turned to Moshe. "Moshe, however…" The edge returned to her voice. "…has decided to study American law and leave the family shop to the old men and poor Sammy! How can you think of politics and law above the family?"

Addie was more shocked to hear Miriam call Papa and Uncle Ehud old men than to hear about Moshe's plans to study law. She felt a pang of sadness for the two brothers. *Uncle Ehud has lost so much these past years, and Papa has suffered, too. All he wants is for our family to be together and safe, just like me.* Sunlight streamed into the room, and Addie watched particles of dust dance in the air, as the words of her brother and sister sunk in.

"Moshe, will you be moving away?" Addie tried to keep the strain out of her voice. Moshe began to pace about the room. The front room suddenly felt tiny, the dreams of Moshe and Miriam too great to fit inside its walls.

"It all depends on Papa—if he'll allow me to stay here and live, or if he throws me out. I'm determined to keep up my studies, even if I'm not able to go to law school for a long time."

Addie felt confused and sad, and a little afraid of being left behind. She'd always assumed Moshe would take over the family business, as a puppy always grows into a dog. The realization that he might attend a university and work somewhere other than the hat shop suddenly struck her. How strange to live among these children who were becoming adults...but not the adults that they were expected to become. *Who will I become when all is said and done?* She thought of Mrs. Raczynski and the Hebrew Ladies Benevolent Society and of Dr. Goldstein's words, then thought of Mama in the kitchen and with her sewing. *Will Mama and Papa accept the person that I decide to become?*

Addie had a sudden urge to make time move backward, to the moment when Uncle Chaim had first arrived from the train station two years ago, surprising them just before the evening meal. Without even taking his hat off, he'd opened up his leather steamer case and rooted around in the bottom of it until he found a small silver tin. The tin held precious German sweets, velvet truffles that Moshe and Miriam swooned over. Addie had never tasted anything like them before, so was most excited by the smooth looking tin and the bright-eyed uncle she'd only heard about from Mama's stories. Her life had sat on even ground then, with each family member playing the part expected of them. David alive. Uncle Chaim sleeping on the sofa. Now, everything was topsy-turvy. Papa was trying so hard to hold onto the reins that pulled the precarious wagon of their family.

Miriam shook her head and wagged her finger at Moshe. "He should throw you out. You're lucky to be a boy and to be the pride of the family and get to take on all that they've worked for. Addie and

I have to marry the right men, have children, and make ourselves useful. It isn't fair." Hot, angry tears streaked down her cheeks, and she left the apartment without a hat or coat or anything at all. Addie wondered if she'd ever come back.

Moshe turned to Addie. "She'll be back. Just wait." He picked up the newspaper and began to thumb through it.

Addie's leg throbbed. *I should go lay back down.* But she felt restless and lonely, with her heart aching for times that had passed. If only she could flash back in time and warn Uncle Ehud of the danger of David's illness or tell Uncle Chaim to keep quiet about the union. These thoughts sloshed about in her mind, as though she were out on a stormy sea.

"Addie." Moshe called her back. "Let's play Elfern, to keep our spirits from sagging." He picked up a deck of cards and began to deal. Addie shifted her leg to a better position. They played cards long into the afternoon, until the orange evening sun poured into the front room window. The game of Elfern required a great deal of concentration, so for a few blissful hours Addie thought only of her bidding strategy and counting cards. At half past five, Mama, Papa, Uncle Ehud, Sammy, and Miriam arrived at the apartment, looking like a flock of mournful sheep, all huddled together and forlorn. Addie was relieved to see Miriam with them, her patch on the family quilt still intact.

Uncle Ehud looked particularly grim and poured himself a glass of something. Sammy ran to Addie, realized that he couldn't sit on her lap because of her hurt leg and buried his face into her neck. Addie could feel his tears against her skin and swallowed hard to keep from crying, too.

"Sammy, pull up a chair and we can play Snap. Moshe and I've been playing cards all afternoon and it's taken my mind off all the sad things."

Sammy wiped his tears away and his face brightened a bit. Moshe smiled at Addie. "Sammy, you take my seat and play. I need to use the washroom."

Papa and Uncle Ehud spoke in solemn-low voices. "Leave the boy and go back to the temple. It's only right and Sammy will be fine with us. Look at Addie playing with him. We'll be all right." Papa's voice sounded hard-rough, like a weathered cobblestone.

"Snap!" Sammy called out, pleased and excited, seeming to forget for the moment that his twin brother was dead. They played several rounds, until someone rapped at the front door. Papa rose from his chair, opened the door and exclaimed loudly. Addie looked up from the game and gasped. There, on the threshold, stood Uncle Chaim.

Twenty-Six

J OSEF, I..." Uncle Chaim stammered, as though he were expecting a blow from Papa. His overcoat looked threadbare and he wore a dark derby pulled low over his brow. "I...I came to say goodbye to Sara and the children. Please allow me that and then I'll be on my way."

Addie stood up on both feet without thinking, then felt a streak of pain through her leg and sat back down on the chair. Mama and Miriam came rushing out of the kitchen when they heard the sound of Uncle Chaim's voice.

"Chaim!" Mama called out and ran to him. Papa stood aside and watched as they embraced. He seemed unsure of what to do or say.

Uncle Chaim looked at Addie, noticed her leg propped up, and his face dropped. "But what's happened to Addie?"

He must think I hurt my leg after helping Michael. Is that why he looks upset? Addie had never even found out what happened to Michael after she helped with his arm. *Did he make it out of Chicago?*

Mama reassured her brother. "Oh, Chaim! She's fine. But it's David...he passed from the consumption." Her voice caught. "Addie went out to fetch the undertaker and collapsed from exhaustion. But the doctor says she'll be all right. Only her leg is bruised from the fall."

Uncle Chaim grabbed the back of a chair to steady himself. "Sara, Josef, I'm so sorry. Where's Ehud?" He saw Sammy at the table and swooped down to pick him up in a great bear hug. Papa look flustered and his face became red, but he didn't move or speak. Sammy clung to Uncle Chaim. The room felt heavy with grief as Uncle Chaim took in the news of David's death.

Finally, Mama spoke. "Ehud's gone to the temple. We've just come from there." She began to dab the tears at the corner of her eyes with her apron. "But Chaim, Chaim...come to say goodbye? Where are you going? Why, oh why must you leave?"

Addie could barely breathe. Here was Uncle Chaim, back in the front room, comforting Sammy and filling the little space with his generous self—this moment she'd hoped and prayed for—and yet now he was speaking of going away again.

"Yes, Sara. It's not safe for me any longer in Chicago. The police are rounding up members of the union and I must leave at once. I'll write, of course, and perhaps we'll be able to see each other again...after some time."

Addie needed to hold onto something, anything that would make her feel attached to the earth and not floating above this terrible nightmare. She reached for her quilt and clutched it tightly in both hands.

"But where will you go?" Mama asked, her voice quavering.

"West. Many of my comrades are going west, where there's work on the railway. I'll write when I've found a place."

Addie swallowed hard. Her throat felt tight and painful. Perhaps he would go to Dakota Territory, as well, and would live near Miriam. Jealousy rose in her like bile and burned her chest.

"But when must you leave, Chaim? Will you at least stay and join us for the evening meal?" Mama glanced at Papa now. Addie couldn't tell if she was afraid of his reaction or was daring him to contradict her. Papa seemed shaken and unsure of himself.

Uncle Chaim addressed Mama. "Next Monday. On the morning train to Omaha."

Papa finally spoke up, looking at the floor and spitting his words out quickly and carefully. "I will go to the temple and join Ehud and return by half past eight." Addie knew, as they all did, that Papa expected Uncle Chaim to be gone by the time he returned. *"Auf wiedersehen,* Chaim."

"And goodbye to you, Josef," said Uncle Chaim.

Papa put on his hat and coat and walked out the door. Addie inhaled deeply, suddenly aware that she had barely taken a breath since her uncle's arrival. Uncle Chaim sat down on a chair with Sammy still clinging to him like a cub, while Mama and Miriam and Moshe, who'd been in the back room, gathered around him and began to ask a million questions. With Papa gone, they spoke freely, and with love and care and concern for their beloved uncle.

"The unions have been weakened," Uncle Chaim explained. "People are turning against us because of the bomb thrown at the police, and they're no longer willing to look at the real problem, which is the treatment of the workers. The riot's been a great blow to our cause." He shook his head. "It might take years to restore the confidence and support of the people."

Addie wanted to ask Uncle Chaim about Michael, but felt tongue-tied and unsure about what was supposed to be kept secret. As though reading her mind, Uncle Chaim told a story about one of his comrades whose arm had been pulled from its socket during the riot but was successfully put back into place with the help of a brave young woman.

Miriam seemed to take particular interest in this story. "But how did she do it?" and "Can you really put an arm back where it belongs, once it's been pulled out?"

Uncle Chaim explained that his friend's arm worked normally again and that he was no longer in pain. His friend had left Chicago two nights before, on the midnight train to St. Louis. "The young woman was extremely brave and kind. None of us can ever thank her enough or forget her kindness." His voice sounded proud-calm.

Addie blushed and looked down at her fingers, afraid that she would betray Uncle Chaim with her bright red cheeks. None of the others noticed her, though, as they were riveted by his stories. Mama decided against fixing a proper meal, as she didn't want to miss a moment with her brother, so Miriam brought in several loaves of bread and a block of cured meat and they ate as though picnicking on the lakefront again.

Papa had given them three final hours to eat and talk with Uncle Chaim and they savored the moments together. They discussed the riot and cried over David. Each family member had secrets to guard. Yet Addie felt closer to her family that evening than she had in many weeks...and would perhaps ever feel again.

Twenty-Seven

THOUGH THE sky still blazed with the colors of sunrise the air already felt thick with summer's impending heat. Addie woke with a start, sensing that something was terribly wrong. The spot where Miriam slept was cold. Mama never allowed Addie to sleep late and, while the extra rest made her limbs feel pleasantly heavy and warm, Addie realized that Mama was trying to soften the blow of what lay ahead. Uncle Chaim would climb aboard a train bound for Nebraska later that morning. From there he would try to make his way further west, perhaps as far as San Francisco. He wanted to put plenty of space between himself and the terrible aftermath of the Haymarket riot. Papa had made it clear that he would never allow Chaim completely back into the family. He could come to Shabbat, and could see Mama and Addie as he wished, but the iciness between the two men would never thaw.

Addie pulled the scratchy, gray blanket over her head and hugged herself. With Uncle Chaim gone there was little chance that Papa would find out how she'd helped Michael. Though she knew now for certain that Papa loved her, she also knew that she didn't agree with many of his opinions. He had a clean, comfortable shop to work in, where he and his brother were their own bosses. Their family had warm beds to sleep in and plenty of good food to eat. They had time to read the newspaper, to play cards together, and to go on picnics at the lakefront.

But Addie had seen the way other people worked and lived, and she had come to understand what Uncle Chaim and the others were fighting for. She would be forced to listen to Papa read the paper aloud every morning and evening as the trial of the Haymarket suspects unfolded. The news would remind her every day of the hole Uncle Chaim had left in the fabric of her family. She dreaded hearing about how many people would be hanged as an example to other union members and anarchists.

Mama would do whatever she could to make Addie comfortable in the apartment. She would save slices of challah for her to eat after returning home from school when she was most ravenous, and she'd try to change the subject if Papa began to rant about politics.

Addie forced herself to sit up in bed, stretching her arms toward the ceiling with the full length of her body. She could almost feel herself growing, and for once felt excited about becoming taller. *Once I grow up, I can travel west to see Uncle Chaim, or start a school for the factory children, or help bring food and clothes to the new immigrants, or even become a doctor. I won't be trapped as Mama is and I'll find meaningful work to do.* Addie felt light and fluttery, as if she could float away on a gust of wind and travel anywhere.

She found Mama staring out the little window in the kitchen and she gave her a hug. "Good morning, Mama." She kissed her cheek. Mama looked at Addie with an unspoken question, surprised by her cheerfulness and affection.

A pile of washed potatoes stood next to the sink and Addie began to peel them. Mama went back to slicing onions and spoke softly to her. "Your Papa has said we may go to the train station to see Chaim off. Don't mention it to him or he might change his mind. We'll meet Chaim at the butcher's after breakfast and take the streetcar down to the station."

Addie nodded. The bubble of hope in her chest deflated a bit as she remembered once again that Uncle Chaim would be leaving for good. *He'll never, ever return to Chicago—with so much unknown and a family that cannot hold him close.* Addie bit her lip and kept peeling.

"You should go and play with Greta this afternoon, Addie. Take your mind off all our worries." Addie hadn't thought of Greta once these last few days, with her blonde curls and warm smile and the mischievous look in her eye, always looking for trouble or fun. *I remember when I thought it was fun to look for trouble, too.*

"Yes, Mama," Addie replied. It would be good to play with Greta, to pretend to be a child again, even if her heart felt worn out. And she could talk to Mrs. Raczynski, too, and find out more about her work.

After eating, Mama and Addie slipped out of the apartment and went quickly down the stairs. Papa'd left early for the hat shop, and Addie guessed that he and Mama needed to avoid each other. Mama grabbed Addie's hand as they reached the street. She'd forgotten how rarely Mama left home, and realized that the noise of the wagons and crowds must be alarming. Mama covered her mouth and nose with her handkerchief and looked down at the ground, unable to take in everything on the streets. Her arthritis made her feet shuffle awkwardly. Addie suddenly had a vision of Mama as a bird, sitting up on her perch most of the day, building and tending her nest, far above the ground below.

They moved slowly across several blocks to the butcher-shop, where Uncle Chaim stood leaning against the front window, reading a paper. He looked up at Addie and grinned. His face lit up and he reached one arm each for Mama and Addie. Addie felt such a strong tugging inside. She could feel the warmth and love for her uncle, and also the terrible emptiness of knowing that she would not see him again for many years...or maybe forever. Mama and Uncle Chaim linked arms, with Addie on his other side, and the three walked toward the streetcar stop.

Mama spoke quickly and without pause. "Please write as often and as much as you can and we'll write, too, and let you know of any danger or any other news, and of course we'll tell you family news as well. I think Miriam's being courted and may marry soon and of course Moshe may choose to go on to college and who knows what will happen with the shop and Ehud and Sammy, but we'll stay in touch." Mama continued without catching a breath. Addie had an urge to reassure her mama, to swaddle her in an embrace that could calm and comfort her threadbare nerves.

A streetcar stopped and Uncle Chaim climbed on first, then pulled out the fare for all three of them. The driver asked if he needed transfers and he answered, "Only two." Addie sighed to herself. She would travel back home alone with Mama, and the two of them would have to hold each other up. She dreaded the burden, realizing how sad Mama would feel without her only brother. They stood very close to each other as the car hurtled down Randolph Street toward downtown. Since Addie rarely rode the cars, she loved to watch the streets move below her while her body stayed perfectly still. She was in a dream, moving through time sideways. Uncle Chaim had his hand on Mama's shoulder and they spoke quietly in German. After twenty minutes they got down from the car and began to walk several blocks to the train station. Suddenly, Uncle Chaim stopped and broke the silence.

"Leave me here. It'll be easier than watching the train leave."

Mama's face fell, but she nodded.

"Come, Addie. We have to say goodbye for now."

A cry stuck in Addie's throat. She covered her mouth with her hands and tears pricked her eyes. Uncle Chaim held her shoulders and looked into her eyes. "Grow tall and proud, like a black walnut tree. Don't be afraid, Addie. Stand up to your full height and show the world who you are." His voice brimmed with hope and pride. But the words did not reach Addie, and would only find her in the years that followed, when she could barely remember what her uncle's face looked like. He turned to Mama, who suddenly seemed small and old.

"I'll write soon. Be well." His voice was crackly-warm and he gave her a short hug and turned to go.

Mama and Addie held onto each other for several minutes. Addie's whole body tensed, as though preparing to fight an enormous grief that threatened to knock her down. They turned back toward the streetcar, arm in arm, with only the promise of their dreams to sustain them.

Epilogue

December 11, 1887

My dear Uncle,

Mama just showed me your letter from the great city of San Francisco. I jumped up and down to hear that you are well and safe. I wish I could ride on your shoulders looking down on the exotic city you describe and the glittering Pacific Ocean. From that high perch, I would be even taller than you, yet still so close.

It has been exactly a month since six men were hung to death for throwing a bomb at the police in the Haymarket Square last year. Mama stayed in the kitchen all that day and fried latkes for a new family at temple and wouldn't talk, even after I begged her to tell me stories of the olden days when you, Mama, Oma and Opa grew potatoes and turnips and raised chickens in Germany. She was sullen and sad, so I filled the kitchen up with my own stories of the people I've been visiting with Mrs. Raczynski every week after school. Oh, Uncle! So many children with sores that won't heal and old women with sad, empty eyes and tired mothers and fathers who limp home late at night smelling of drink. My heart feels heavy sometimes on those afternoons. Still, the boys and girls want to play pat-a-cake and hide-and-seek and laugh heartily when I pull my foolish faces. And they cry over the food we bring them, and thank us so much that I blush with embarrassment.

Mama and Papa won't talk much about Mr. Parsons and Mr. Spies and the other men who were hung, but I think Papa is pleased that they were punished with death. He calls them "dynamite orators" and "bloody anarchists" and blames them for Americans not coming into the shop as much as they used to. Now it's mostly the Germans and Dutch and Belgians and Prussians who buy our hats. Even though there are so many of us Europeans all over the city, Papa says we aren't welcome anymore and it's best to try to pass as Americans. He thinks the anarchists poisoned America against us. At school, I soften my voice to sound less German, which is easy because I'm good at playacting and oration. I feel worst for Mama, since her accent is so thick and her American is chipped, like an old tea cup.

Mrs. Raczynski told me all about the anarchists and their trial. She's not afraid to talk about them and calls it exercising her American right of free speech. I'm careful not to pass along all her words to Mama and Papa, or else I might not be allowed to join her anymore. Mrs. R says that the anarchists are martyrs and received an unfair trial and were killed to make the police look good and give a rest to all the upheaval. I'm not sure I understand what a martyr is, but think she must mean that they didn't deserve to die and yet the workers feel someone cared enough to fight for them, so their deaths were good in a backwards way. Mrs. R likes to say that whoever digs a pit for others will fall into it themselves, which I think must be a warning to the judge and jury.

All the people on the jury were American-born and biased against the immigrants, which Mrs. R says is not fair or right or American, and she even says that some of the evidence brought against the men was made up or exaggerated. She doesn't believe they threw the bomb at all and wears a little pin on her dress protesting the unfair trial. I steal glimpses at any newspapers I can find—the *Chicago Tribune* and the *Arbeiter-Zeitung*, all with bold headlines about the fearful European immigrant anarchists endangering capitalism or the vicious companies stealing the workingmen's lifeblood. So many letters and words crowding over the papers and into the minds and onto the tongues of everyone in Chicago!

I am glad to have Mrs. R to listen to, since Moshe has been gone for over a year. Mama must have written to you that he started studying at the Maurer School of Law in Indiana last year and didn't even come home in the summer because he got a job with a local judge and wanted to save his railway fare. Moshe only writes us a bit, as he's so busy with his books, but promises to come home for Passover in March.

Miriam's been helping Papa at the shop and Papa's been teaching her to keep the money ledger and fill out orders and talk to the lady customers about the latest fashions. Miriam loves to preen over the ladies and keep the place tidy and calls the shop her element, which of course makes Papa crow like a rooster. Her suitor is in Dakota Territory, though Miriam doesn't mention him anymore and sometimes her eyes are puffy and red in the morning.

Uncle Ehud and Sammy moved into Widow Adler's apartment after she died last June. Having no relatives to speak of, Uncle kept the widow's old furniture that was brought over in the '40s from Germany, including an old walnut desk that Papa says was used by Ferdinand the First! Sammy seems reluctant to grow, though his body keeps stretching up in spite of himself. Sometimes I wonder if he's waiting for David to catch up to him.

Oh, Uncle! I must end my letter with the words left unspoken in my heart. I wish you would come home to Chicago now! With the Haymarket trial over and the anarchist martyrs hung, we all pray that the fear and terror of the past two years is behind us. Many of the companies have agreed to an eight-hour workday after all, though the railway owners still haven't budged. I won't beg, but felt I must tell you that Chicago has quieted again, at least for the time being, and that Mama and I long for your return every day.

With love from your little bear, Addie

Acknowledgments

I AM SO grateful for all the help and support I received while writing this book. Specifically, Emily Victorson of Allium Press and my editor, Amanda Gersh, who held my hand through the laborious process of revision. My dear friends: Jess, Ingrid, Becca, Khaliqa, Gabriella, Becky, Eva, Lydia, Rosie, Dana, Trever, and Trace. The incredible writers in my life, who provide me with advice, inspiration and courage: Shelley, Rachel, Heather, Emily, Leni, and my uncles Henry and Richard. My writing group: Kirsten, Megan, Sprig, Heather, and Laurie. Matty: for giving me the idea to write about the Haymarket. My earliest readers: Jennifer and Jo Powell, who encouraged me when the book was still in its roughest form. My long-lost friend Ginny, who became one of Addie's greatest advocates. The young readers who participated in my read-aloud tea parties and provided invaluable feedback: Ocean, Hannah, Siana, and Maggie. And especially my sister/ writer Lucinda, who suggested that I try writing my favorite genre, and Melissa, my writing teacher and companion along the way. My siblings, Kathy, Johnny, Ben, and Cecily, who share their creativity and praise with generous hearts. My wonderful mother, Ann Macrory, whose curiosity and sense of justice and service inspired the character of Addie. My father, Patrick Macrory, who brought me the legacy of a family of writers and has always cheered me along the way. My husband, Tom Powell—my very own Chicago anarchist, the rock of my life.

This novel is not intended to be a definitive resource on the Haymarket Affair. Instead, it provides a window into that time in Chicago's history through the experiences of a young Jewish girl.

If you would like more information about the Haymarket Affair, and Jewish life in Chicago during that time, please explore the resources provided in the companion guide available on the Allium Press website at www.alliumpress.com/our-books/city-of-grit-and-gold/. In the guide you will also find questions that will help you have a discussion about the book, along with a list of similar novels that you might enjoy.

For images related to *City of Grit and Gold*
—of Chicago in the 1880s, the Haymarket Affair, hats,
sweatshops and their workers, etc.—
visit our Pinterest page for this book at
www.pinterest.com/alliumpress/city-of-grit-and-gold.

ALSO PUBLISHED BY ALLIUM PRESS OF CHICAGO

Visit our website for more information:
www.alliumpress.com

THE EMILY CABOT MYSTERIES
Frances McNamara

Death at the Fair

The 1893 World's Columbian Exposition provides a vibrant backdrop for the first book in the series. Emily Cabot, one of the first women graduate students at the University of Chicago, is eager to prove herself in the emerging field of sociology. While she is busy exploring the Exposition with her family and friends, her colleague, Dr. Stephen Chapman, is accused of murder. Emily sets out to search for the truth behind the crime, but is thwarted by the gamblers, thieves, and corrupt politicians who are ever-present in Chicago. A lynching that occurred in the dead man's past leads Emily to seek the assistance of the black activist Ida B. Wells.

◆

Death at Hull House

After Emily Cabot is expelled from the University of Chicago, she finds work at Hull House, the famous settlement established by Jane Addams. There she quickly becomes involved in the political and social problems of the immigrant community. But when a man who works for a sweatshop owner is murdered in the Hull House parlor, Emily must determine whether one of her colleagues is responsible, or whether the real reason for the murder is revenge for a past tragedy in her own family. As a smallpox epidemic spreads through the impoverished west side of Chicago, the very existence of the settlement is threatened and Emily finds herself in jeopardy from both the deadly disease and a killer.

THE EMILY CABOT MYSTERIES
Frances McNamara

Death at Pullman

A model town at war with itself . . . George Pullman created an ideal community for his railroad car workers, complete with every amenity they could want or need. But when hard economic times hit in 1894, lay-offs follow and the workers can no longer pay their rent or buy food at the company store. Starving and desperate, they turn against their once benevolent employer. Emily Cabot and her friend Dr. Stephen Chapman bring much needed food and medical supplies to the town, hoping they can meet the immediate needs of the workers and keep them from resorting to violence. But when one young worker—suspected of being a spy—is murdered, and a bomb plot comes to light, Emily must race to discover the truth behind a tangled web of family and company alliances.

◆

Death at Woods Hole

Exhausted after the tumult of the Pullman Strike of 1894, Emily Cabot is looking forward to a restful summer visit to Cape Cod. She has plans to collect "beasties" for the Marine Biological Laboratory, alongside other visiting scientists from the University of Chicago. She also hopes to enjoy romantic clambakes with Dr. Stephen Chapman, although they must keep an important secret from their friends. But her summer takes a dramatic turn when she finds a dead man floating in a fish tank. In order to solve his murder she must first deal with dueling scientists, a testy local sheriff, the theft of a fortune, and uncooperative weather.

THE EMILY CABOT MYSTERIES
Frances McNamara

Death at Chinatown

In the summer of 1896, amateur sleuth Emily Cabot meets two young
Chinese women who have recently received medical degrees. She is
inspired to make an important decision about her own life when she
learns about the difficult choices they have made in order to pursue
their careers. When one of the women is accused of poisoning a Chinese
herbalist, Emily once again finds herself in the midst of a murder
investigation. But, before the case can be solved, she must first settle
a serious quarrel with her husband, help quell a political uprising, and
overcome threats against her family. Timeless issues, such as restrictions
on immigration, the conflict between Western and Eastern medicine,
and women's struggle to balance family and work, are woven seamlessly
throughout this mystery set in Chicago's original Chinatown.

◆

Death at the Paris Exposition

In the sixth Emily Cabot Mystery, the intrepid amateur sleuth's journey
once again takes her to a world's fair—the Paris Exposition of 1900.
Chicago socialite Bertha Palmer has been named the only female U. S.
commissioner to the Exposition and she enlists Emily's services as her
social secretary. Their visit to the House of Worth for the fitting of a
couture gown is interrupted by the theft of Mrs. Palmer's famous pearl
necklace. Before that crime can be solved, several young women meet
untimely deaths and a member of the Palmer's inner circle is accused
of the crimes. As Emily races to clear the family name she encounters
jealous society ladies, American heiresses seeking titled European
husbands, and more luscious gowns and priceless jewels. Along the way,
she takes refuge from the tumult at the country estate of Impressionist
painter Mary Cassatt. In between her work and sleuthing, she is able
to share the Art Nouveau delights of the Exposition, and the enduring
pleasures of the City of Light, with her husband and their young children.

Beautiful Dreamer
Joan Naper

Chicago in 1900 is bursting with opportunity, and Kitty Coakley is determined to make the most of it. The youngest of seven children born to Irish immigrants, she has little interest in becoming simply a housewife. Inspired by her entrepreneurial Aunt Mabel, who runs a millinery boutique at Marshall Field's, Kitty aspires to become an independent, modern woman. After her music teacher dashes her hopes of becoming a professional singer, she refuses to give up her dreams of a career. But when she is courted by not one, but two young men, her resolve is tested. Irish-Catholic Brian is familiar and has the approval of her traditional, working-class family. But wealthy, Protestant Henry, who is a young architect in Daniel Burnham's office, provides an entrée for Kitty into another, more exciting world. Will she sacrifice her ambitions and choose a life with one of these men?

◆

Company Orders
David J. Walker

Even a good man may feel driven to sign on with the devil. Paul Clark is a Catholic priest who's been on the fast track to becoming a bishop. But he suddenly faces a heart-wrenching problem, when choices he made as a young man come roaring back into his life. A mysterious woman, who claims to be with "an agency of the federal government," offers to solve his problem. But there's a price to pay—Father Clark must undertake some very un-priestly actions. An attack in a Chicago alley…a daring escape from a Mexican jail…and a fight to the death in a Guyanese jungle…all these, and more, must be survived in order to protect someone he loves. This priest is about to learn how much easier it is to preach love than to live it.

Set the Night on Fire
Libby Fischer Hellmann

Someone is trying to kill Lila Hilliard. During the Christmas holidays she returns from running errands to find her family home in flames, her father and brother trapped inside. Later, she is attacked by a mysterious man on a motorcycle. . . and the threats don't end there. As Lila desperately tries to piece together who is after her and why, she uncovers information about her father's past in Chicago during the volatile days of the late 1960s . . . information he never shared with her, but now threatens to destroy her. Part thriller, part historical novel, and part love story, *Set the Night on Fire* paints an unforgettable portrait of Chicago during a turbulent time: the riots at the Democratic Convention . . . the struggle for power between the Black Panthers and SDS . . . and a group of young idealists who tried to change the world.

◆

A Bitter Veil
Libby Fischer Hellmann

It all began with a line of Persian poetry . . . Anna and Nouri, both studying in Chicago, fall in love despite their very different backgrounds. Anna, who has never been close to her parents, is more than happy to return with Nouri to his native Iran, to be embraced by his wealthy family. Beginning their married life together in 1978, their world is abruptly turned upside down by the overthrow of the Shah and the rise of the Islamic Republic. Under the Ayatollah Khomeini and the Republican Guard, life becomes increasingly restricted and Anna must learn to exist in a transformed world, where none of the familiar Western rules apply. Random arrests and torture become the norm, women are required to wear hijab, and Anna discovers that she is no longer free to leave the country. As events reach a fevered pitch, Anna realizes that nothing is as she thought, and no one can be trusted. . .not even her husband.

Her Mother's Secret
Barbara Garland Polikoff

Fifteen-year-old Sarah, the daughter of Jewish immigrants, wants nothing more than to become an artist. But as she spreads her wings she must come to terms with the secrets that her family is only beginning to share with her. Replete with historical details that vividly evoke the Chicago of the 1890s, this moving coming-of-age story is set against the backdrop of a vibrant, turbulent city. Sarah moves between two very different worlds—the colorful immigrant neighborhood surrounding Hull House and the sophisticated, elegant World's Columbian Exposition. This novel eloquently captures the struggles of a young girl as she experiences the timeless emotions of friendship, family turmoil, loss…and first love.

A companion guide to *Her Mother's Secret*
is available at www.alliumpress.com. In the guide you will find photographs of places mentioned in the novel, along with discussion questions, a list of read-alikes, and resources for further exploration of Sarah's time and place.

Shall We Not Revenge
D. M. Pirrone

In the harsh early winter months of 1872, while Chicago is still smoldering from the Great Fire, Irish Catholic detective Frank Hanley is assigned the case of a murdered Orthodox Jewish rabbi. His investigation proves difficult when the neighborhood's Yiddish-speaking residents, wary of outsiders, are reluctant to talk. But when the rabbi's headstrong daughter, Rivka, unexpectedly offers to help Hanley find her father's killer, the detective receives much more than the break he was looking for.

Their pursuit of the truth draws Rivka and Hanley closer together and leads them to a relief organization run by the city's wealthy movers and shakers. Along the way, they uncover a web of political corruption, crooked cops, and well-buried ties to two notorious Irish thugs from Hanley's checkered past. Even after he is kicked off the case, stripped of his badge, and thrown in jail, Hanley refuses to quit. With a personal vendetta to settle for an innocent life lost, he is determined to expose a complicated criminal scheme, not only for his own sake, but for Rivka's as well.

◆

For You Were Strangers
D. M. Pirrone

On a spring morning in 1872, former Civil War officer Ben Champion is discovered dead in his Chicago bedroom—a bayonet protruding from his back. What starts as a routine case for Detective Frank Hanley soon becomes anything but, as his investigation into Champion's life turns up hidden truths best left buried. Meanwhile, Rivka Kelmansky's long-lost brother, Aaron, arrives on her doorstep, along with his mulatto wife and son. Fugitives from an attack by night riders, Aaron and his family know too much about past actions that still threaten powerful men—

defective guns provided to Union soldiers, and an 1864 conspiracy to establish Chicago as the capital of a Northwest Confederacy. Champion had his own connection to that conspiracy, along with ties to a former slave now passing as white and an escaped Confederate guerrilla bent on vengeance, any of which might have led to his death. Hanley and Rivka must untangle this web of circumstances, amid simmering hostilities still present seven years after the end of the Civil War, as they race against time to solve the murder, before the secrets of bygone days claim more victims.

◆

Honor Above All
J. Bard-Collins

Pinkerton agent Garrett Lyons arrives in Chicago in 1882, close on the trail of the person who murdered his partner. He encounters a vibrant city that is striving ever upwards, full of plans to construct new buildings that will "scrape the sky." In his quest for the truth Garrett stumbles across a complex plot involving counterfeit government bonds, fierce architectural competition, and painful reminders of his military past. Along the way he seeks the support and companionship of his friends—elegant Charlotte, who runs an upscale poker game for the city's elite, and up-and-coming architect Louis Sullivan. Rich with historical details that bring early 1880s Chicago to life, this novel will appeal equally to mystery fans, history buffs, and architecture enthusiasts.

The Reason for Time
Mary Burns

Whole minutes passed when I didn't think of my man and the swimming lesson set up for the next day, if no one was murdered before then, or the cars stopped, or a bomb go off somewhere...

On a hot, humid Monday afternoon in July 1919, Maeve Curragh watches as a blimp plunges from the sky and smashes into a downtown Chicago bank building. It is the first of ten extraordinary days in Chicago history that will forever change the course of her life.

Racial tensions mount as soldiers return from the battlefields of Europe and the Great Migration brings new faces to the city, culminating in violent race riots. Each day the young Irish immigrant, a catalogue order clerk for the Chicago Magic Company, devours the news of a metropolis where cultural pressures are every bit as febrile as the weather. But her interest in the headlines wanes when she catches the eye of a charming streetcar conductor.

Maeve's singular voice captures the spirit of a young woman living through one of Chicago's most turbulent periods. Seamlessly blending fact with fiction, Mary Burns weaves an evocative tale of how an ordinary life can become inextricably linked with history.

CPSIA information can be obtained
at www.ICGtesting.com
Printed in the USA
FFOW02n0824150517
35473FF